The Vanishing Statue

Read all the mysteries in the
NANCY DREW DIARIES

#1 Curse of the *Arctic Star*

#2 Strangers on a Train

#3 Mystery of the Midnight Rider

#4 Once Upon a Thriller

#5 Sabotage at Willow Woods

#6 Secret at Mystic Lake

#7 The Phantom of Nantucket

#8 The Magician's Secret

#9 The Clue at Black Creek Farm

#10 A Script for Danger

#11 The Red Slippers

#12 The Sign in the Smoke

#13 The Ghost of Grey Fox Inn

#14 Riverboat Roulette

#15 The Professor and the Puzzle

#16 The Haunting on Heliotrope Lane

A Nancy Drew Christmas

#17 Famous Mistakes

#18 The Stolen Show

#19 Hidden Pictures

Coming soon:

#21 Danger at the Iron Dragon

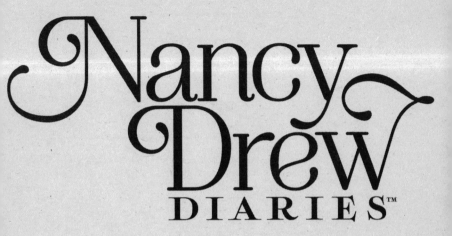

Nancy Drew
DIARIES™

The Vanishing Statue

#20

CAROLYN KEENE

𝒜laddin

NEW YORK LONDON TORONTO SYDNEY NEW DELHI

ALADDIN

An imprint of Simon & Schuster Children's Publishing Division

1230 Avenue of the Americas, New York, New York 10020

First Aladdin paperback edition May 2020

Text copyright © 2020 by Simon & Schuster, Inc.

Cover illustration copyright © 2020 by Erin McGuire

Also available in an Aladdin hardcover edition.

All rights reserved, including the right of reproduction in whole or in part in any form.

ALADDIN and related logo are registered trademarks of Simon & Schuster, Inc.

NANCY DREW, NANCY DREW DIARIES, and related logo are trademarks of Simon & Schuster, Inc.

For information about special discounts for bulk purchases, please contact Simon & Schuster Special Sales at 1-866-506-1949 or business@simonandschuster.com.

The Simon & Schuster Speakers Bureau can bring authors to your live event. For more information or to book an event contact the Simon & Schuster Speakers Bureau at 1-866-248-3049 or visit our website at www.simonspeakers.com.

Series designed by Karin Paprocki

Cover designed by Heather Palisi

Interior designed by Mike Rosamilia

The text of this book was set in Adobe Caslon Pro.

Manufactured in the United States of America 0420 OFF

2 4 6 8 10 9 7 5 3 1

Library of Congress Cataloging-in-Publication Data

Names: Keene, Carolyn, author.

Title: The vanishing statue / by Carolyn Keene.

Description: First Aladdin hardcover/paperback edition. | New York : Aladdin, 2020. |

Series: Nancy Drew diaries; #20 | Audience: Ages 8-12 | Audience: Grades 4-6 |

Summary: While attending a fancy party hosted by Duchess Strickland, a wealthy philanthropist who owns a priceless art collection, teenaged Nancy Drew finds a new mystery to investigate when the goddess statue disappears.

Identifiers: LCCN 2019026964 (print) | LCCN 2019026965 (eBook) |

ISBN 9781534421783 (paperback) | ISBN 9781534421790 (hardcover) |

ISBN 9781534421806 (eBook)

Subjects: CYAC: Mystery and detective stories. | Art—Fiction.

Classification: LCC PZ7.K23 Van 2020 (print) | LCC PZ7.K23 (eBook) | DDC [Fic]—dc23

LC record available at https://lccn.loc.gov/2019026964

LC eBook record available at https://lccn.loc.gov/2019026965

Contents

CHAPTER ONE   A Mysterious Invitation   1

CHAPTER TWO   The Masked Dancer   16

CHAPTER THREE   Diana Disappears   36

CHAPTER FOUR   Artsy Characters   51

CHAPTER FIVE   A Glamorous Fraud   67

CHAPTER SIX   Arriving in Style   81

CHAPTER SEVEN   The Blank Wall   102

CHAPTER EIGHT   The Empty Pedestal   121

CHAPTER NINE   The Duchess's
Announcement   137

CHAPTER TEN   Lights Out   148

CHAPTER ELEVEN   The Strickland
Family Business   162

CHAPTER TWELVE   A Low-Speed Chase   186

CHAPTER THIRTEEN   The Artist Revealed   204

Dear Diary,

YOU MIGHT THINK RIVER HEIGHTS IS a pretty average town: not too big, not too small, with enough new businesses popping up and strangers passing through to keep life interesting. But this year, the town is throwing our first annual Art Week. The River Heights Museum of Fine Art will have free admission after five p.m., and there's going to be a parade and a new art gallery opening in East River Heights. The city hired artists to paint murals in the alleyways downtown. The streets are suddenly full of visitors with interesting outfits and even more interesting haircuts.

I think all the arty visitors are inspiring the locals to be more creative too. Yesterday, George and I watched a woman spray-paint a huge golden dragon onto the side of the hardware store. My ordinary town already seems more colorful. I hope some of our unusual visitors take a liking to River Heights and decide to stay.

The Vanishing Statue

CHAPTER ONE

A Mysterious Invitation

USUALLY I'D BE HAPPY TO HEAR THE latest River Heights gossip from one of my best friends, Bess Marvin. But not when she called my cell at eight a.m. on a Saturday, when I was trying to sleep in. I answered on the fourth ring, still half dreaming about a mystery in a haunted castle where the final clue was just out of reach. . . .

Bess's musical laughter startled me awake. "Nancy, I can hear you snoring! Wake up! You have to check your mailbox right now."

"Bess, it's too early. The mail hasn't even been

delivered yet. Ms. Vandra comes at eleven on Saturdays."

"This is *special mail*, Nancy. Hand delivered by members of her staff."

"Staff? Whose staff? What are you talking about?"

"Her staff. Gosh, I'd love to have people to order around. She probably sits on her throne all day just telling different people what to do. . . ."

I groaned and rolled out of bed.

"Bess, you're not making sense. If you'd just give me a minute, I'll go get the 'special mail' and figure it out for myself."

I rubbed the sleep from my eyes, pulled on a robe and slippers, and headed out into the chilly morning to check the mailbox. I put Bess on speakerphone and let her keep chattering away. I knew even if I told her to buzz off and let me sleep, she'd call back until I did as she said. Bess could be very persistent.

"I'm thinking something chic and black with architectural elements. Or maybe a glamorous take on the tuxedo, with a sparkly cape! I can't wait, Nancy. It's going to be fabulous!"

"All right. Slow down. Let me see if there's anything in here. . . ." I rummaged around in the gloomy mailbox, keeping watch for spiders. At the back I found three small gold-colored envelopes. One was addressed to me: MISS NANCY DREW. The second was to my father, CARSON DREW, ESQ. And the third was for our housekeeper, Hannah Gruen.

"Did you get the invitation?" asked Bess, unable to contain herself. "You did! You got it! Nancy, it's the party of the year, and we're invited!"

"What are we invited to?"

I tore open the envelope addressed to me. The invitation inside was printed in gold ink on thick, cream-colored paper; I had to tilt the paper at just the right angle in order to catch enough light to read it by.

Please accept this invitation to a Celebration
of the Arts next Saturday evening, March
18, at the Strickland mansion on Regent's

Hill Road, at six o'clock. Suitable dress politely requested. This is a one-time-only event. It will not be repeated.

Regent's Hill Road winds along the ridge on the north side of town. It's mostly hiking trails and horse farms out there. I didn't know much about the Strickland mansion, just that it was the home of a wealthy but reclusive widow who'd had something to do with the arts in River Heights years ago. Now, all of a sudden, I was being invited to a grand party at that very mansion.

Before I had time to wonder about the reason for the invitation, Bess said, "So, our hostess is pretty eccentric. Nobody's allowed to use her first name. She only answers to "Duchess" because her husband's name was Duke. That's just according to rumor, though. She hasn't been seen in town for ten years, not since her husband died."

"So why would she break her silence now?"

"No idea, but I'll tell you one thing. That mansion

must have the best view in all of River Heights. And I, for one, intend to savor that view. Maybe strike a few poses for the photographers, show off my fabulous gown . . . Remember that sculpture class I took last summer? With that cute TA?"

"Oh, the infamous Sven Svenstein? You wouldn't stop talking about him after he gave you that book on female performance artists."

"I'm going to ask him to be my date. What about *you*, my gumshoe friend?"

"I'm definitely going, mystery or not!"

"That's all I wanted to hear. You go back to bed now, Nancy. I'll see you later at the Slay Gallery opening. I have to hang up so I can start making my vision board. I haven't even settled on a color palette. . . ."

Of course, once you've been out to the mailbox early in the morning and received a mysterious invitation, it can be very hard to fall asleep again. I gave up on returning to my dream of the haunted castle and wandered downstairs to the kitchen, where I found

Hannah making coffee and whistling a merry tune.

"Wow, look who's up early! Are you hungry? I can make French toast. . . ."

"Oh, yes please!" I exclaimed. Hannah's French toast is heavenly, topped with a cloud of her home-made whipped cream and strawberries. Lately she'd been adding extra toppings like cinnamon and shaved Mexican chocolate, even a little chili powder. I loved her classic French toast, but her creative new flavors made my mouth water!

"Hannah, did you see a stranger come by this morning to deliver some mail?"

"No, why?"

"We just got these fancy invitations," I explained, and handed over the one addressed to her.

After she'd opened the envelope and read the invitation, I asked her, "Do you know anything about this Duchess person?"

"All I know is that she's very wealthy and was a big patron of the arts before her husband died. Your father will probably know more." She paused, then added, "If

I met the Duchess, I might say something silly and make her faint dead away!"

I laughed. Hannah was one of my favorite people to talk to. She was always so warm and down-to-earth. I couldn't imagine anyone not getting along with her.

"I'd better get started on this French toast," she said. "It will be my greatest masterpiece yet! Meanwhile, would you take this to your father for me?"

Without waiting for my answer, Hannah handed me a tray with our silver coffee service. I propped the golden envelope against the mug where my dad would be sure to see it. This would be the perfect opportunity to learn more about the Duchess of River Heights.

Entering my dad's study, I sang, "Good morning!" in my cheeriest voice. That wasn't my normal greeting, but Bess's enthusiasm was infectious. I, too, was imagining the perfect party dress. I couldn't wait to meet artists and visitors from the big city, eat canapés, gaze at paintings, and talk about lofty ideas. And I assumed there'd be dancing.

"Morning, Nancy," Dad mumbled, hardly looking up from his paperwork. I filled his mug and handed it to him. He sipped greedily, closing his eyes. I'll never understand his obsession with black coffee. I poured myself a mug, added plenty of cream, and took a sip. Much better.

"Dad, something came in the mail for you. Don't you want to open it?"

"What's that? Oh, I'm sorry. I don't know where my mind is this morning. Intellectual property law is a real rat's nest. I hate to say it, but I may be in over my head with this case. It's so difficult to prove an idea is original or who thought of it first. Promise me you'll always make sure you get the credit you're due for your hard detective work. Don't let anyone undersell your talents."

"Don't worry. There's no one in River Heights who could solve a mystery as creatively as your daughter."

"Don't I know it." Dad chuckled and slit the golden envelope with an antique letter opener. "Anyway, I could use a break from these papers. . . . Let's see what we have here. An invitation to the Strickland house! Well. I haven't been invited there in years, not since I was a young man, even before I met your mother. I still remember two exquisite paintings the Stricklands had hanging by the staircase—portraits of two children smiling, but their eyes looked sad. All during dinner, I couldn't stop thinking about them. Who were those kids? What had upset them? Who was the painter? I was too shy to ask. Hey, maybe you can find out for me, my darling sleuth."

"Who are the Stricklands?"

"Mr. and Mrs. Strickland threw fabulous parties to raise money for their favorite causes. They helped fund the construction of the River Heights Museum of Fine Art, and they bought nearly half the books in the public library. They were pillars of the River Heights art world, back when River Heights *had* an art world."

"How could one couple have such a big impact on the entire town?"

"Money talks, Nancy. Most wealthy people think of art as a tool to make more money. But I don't think that's what drove the Stricklands. Duke Strickland made his fortune selling lace and ribbons, then cat toys, then bottled teas and tinctures. He was an innovator, River Heights's very own Thomas Edison. Duke was a dear old man, and he was very generous with his money. His wife, the Duchess, filled their house with beautiful art and sculptures. She loved to invite art students to study her collection, and she'd give tours of the mansion."

"So what happened? Why did the Stricklands stop supporting the arts?"

"Duke had a long, terrible illness. While he was in the hospital, the parties stopped and the donations dried up. All the wonderful artsy people who used to visit River Heights stopped coming. When Duke passed away—oh, it must have been about ten years ago—the Duchess was heartbroken. She'd just lost her husband, and not only that, but she must have felt that the artistic community she'd built over the years had abandoned her.

"She disappeared from public life. She vanished into that big mansion and stopped speaking to anyone, even her own family. And gradually, all the artists moved away to big cities."

"Why did the artists leave?" I asked.

"Big cities have more opportunity for artists. Without the Stricklands, River Heights couldn't support the galleries and studios the artists needed to survive."

"So why would the Duchess open her home now?"

"It does seem peculiar," my dad agreed. "Maybe the River Heights Art Week encouraged her. Maybe she's seen some of the new murals and the artists visiting town. Maybe she thinks River Heights is ready to bloom again." Dad took a pensive sip of his coffee.

"Now I'm really curious," I said. "There's no way I'm going to miss the Duchess's party."

"Wouldn't it be wonderful to see her collection again? I wonder if she still has those haunting portraits. Too bad I won't be able to see for myself. The trial for this case is a week from Monday, and it looks like I'll have to spend the entire weekend beforehand preparing. You'll have to pay extra close attention and report everything back to me afterward."

"You know I always do, Dad, but I'm sorry you're not coming," I said as I slipped out of the room, leaving him to his books.

I didn't wait even five minutes before calling Ned. He'd been up for an hour already. I knew he liked to stay in bed and read every morning. I liked that he was studious and quiet, but I had to admit my boyfriend was a little nerdy.

"Hey, Nancy!"

"Ned! Have you heard about the Duchess's party? It's next Saturday, and I want you to be my date. If you don't have an invitation, Dad says you can use his. What do you say? Are you free?"

I heard crackling on the line. Ned probably had a bad connection. That, or he'd rolled over on his phone.

"Nancy? Nancy, I can't go! I'm being kidnapped!"

"Who is it this time?" I asked. "Smugglers? Jewel thieves? A disgruntled magician?"

"The kidnapper . . . is your father. He hired me to help research intellectual property law for this new plagiarism case. I'll be buried in law books all week. I can't go to the party. I wouldn't be any fun."

"Oh no, Ned! I'll have a word with Dad. He'll have to give in. This isn't just any party! And who knows? Maybe a mystery will pop up."

"With artistic types, there's always a mystery. Last night, I was reading about a Renaissance printmaker called Albrecht Dürer who sued another artist for carving duplicates of his wooden printing blocks. The court ruled that the man could go on making the duplicate blocks as long as he didn't include an artist's monogram. After that, Dürer started printing a warning at the front of all his books. I have the quote right here.

"It says: 'Hold! You crafty ones, strangers to work, and pilferers of other men's brains. Think not rashly to lay your thievish hands upon my works. Beware! Know you not that I have a grant from the most glorious Emperor Maximillian, that not one throughout the imperial dominion shall be allowed to print or sell fictitious imitations of these engravings? Listen! And bear in mind that if you do so, through spite or through covetousness, not only will your goods be confiscated, but your bodies also placed in mortal danger.'"

"Mortal danger! That's strong stuff."

"Artists have to be crafty to protect their work. It's much easier to steal an idea than to make one up yourself," said Ned.

"Promise you'll try to join us at the party, at least for a little while?"

"I promise I'll try."

"You work too much, sweet Ned," I said, making sure he could tell I was pouting.

"*You* work too much, Detective Drew."

"That's not true! I'm attending this party strictly as a civilian. A civilian who wants to dance with her cute boyfriend."

"I'm sorry, Nance! I promise I'll take you dancing another time."

"Fine, but I am determined to enjoy myself at the Duchess's party, sans date if I have to!"

"You'll make the best of it. You always do."

"I'll miss you!" I said before hanging up.

I could smell a golden, toasty aroma wafting up from the kitchen. My French toast was ready. As I got to the table, Hannah laid a final sprig of mint on top of a voluminous mound of soft pink cream.

"Raspberries," she said, grinning ear to ear.

CHAPTER TWO

The Masked Dancer

THAT AFTERNOON, BESS AND I MET AT THE new gallery, located in a large concrete building tucked away in an old strip mall at the far fringes of East River Heights, nestled between used car dealerships and tire shops. The storefront had two huge picture windows printed with bright pink vinyl letters that read SLAY GALLERY. We'd been invited to the grand opening and a special performance later that day by two artists who called themselves the Goddess Collective. Bess led me around to the back of the building, where an unmarked gray door led to a warren of artists' studios.

Sven Svenstein, the art student Bess had met, had suggested we visit his studio before the gallery opening. He told Bess he'd give us a sneak peek at his installation in progress. George (my other best friend, and Bess's cousin) had said she was too busy to join us, but I think she just didn't want to. She's never approved of her cousin's crushes, and Sven was a particularly odd one. Bess told me the last time they all hung out together, Sven and George had gotten into a huge fight about whether technology made art better or worse. Since then, George had been trying to avoid anywhere Sven might show his face. But she'd agreed to meet us later at the gallery opening.

Sven was gangly, pale, and thin, with intense gray eyes and a shock of white-blond hair. He always dressed in colorful leotards and refused to walk normally. Some days he only skipped; other days he walked on tiptoes or backward, bumping into people on the street. Sven did not say goodbye to anyone. He preferred to simply disappear, catapulting out of sight the minute you were distracted. When Bess and I had seen him perform at the college a few weeks ago, she'd fallen madly in like with Sven's gray eyes and his ability to make himself the center of attention. I could understand that. Bess could be quite dramatic herself. Maybe they *were* a good match.

Given that my date was unavailable, I was thinking of going with George. She'd also gotten an invitation but immediately lost it in the chaos of her room.

When we got to the studio door labeled with Sven's name, we knocked, but no one answered. I tried the knob and the door swung open, revealing a cavernous concrete space scattered with old telephones, printers, fax machines, paper shredders, and other broken electronics. In the center of the room, Sven had built a giant pyramid of TV sets. The TVs were all showing sections of a different image—the arms, legs, and torso of a faceless man in a bright yellow jumpsuit. The TV where his face should've been was running old *Tom and Jerry* cartoons. I noticed that the televisions didn't have screens except for the head. What at first looked like an image was actually a three-dimensional sculpture positioned inside each of the sets. The construction was clever enough, I thought, but what was it trying to say?

I'd moved closer, trying to find a clue as to the meaning, when the hand in one of the sets suddenly *waved*.

I jumped, but Bess giggled as the TV playing cartoons rose slowly to reveal a very real and three-dimensional face grinning back at us. That wasn't a sculpture inside the pyramid—it was Sven!

I stumbled back but managed to regain my balance. Sven's stunt had shaken me a little. Crossing my arms, I waited for him to explain himself.

He clambered out of the pyramid and took a bow. His yellow jumpsuit was the exact color of scrambled eggs.

Bess applauded, starry-eyed. "It's magnificent," she said.

Magnificent? To me, Sven's art felt more like a dirty trick.

"You must not think so much, Nancy Drew," he said, noticing I hadn't joined in with the praise. "Art is not a mystery. Art is entertainment. An artist writes his name in flashing lights in letters a hundred feet high! Only through spectacle can anyone see the truth. Take this building, for example. It was once a supermarket. Now it is a market of ideas."

Sven's face assumed a serious and businesslike expression as he offered his hand for me to shake. But when I reached out, he grabbed hold of my wrist and spun me around and around, faster and faster. He was stronger than he looked in his jumpsuit, all skinny muscle. I struggled, but he held me tight.

"Sven, stop!"

"Let her go, Sven," Bess cried. "That's not nice."

"Art is not nice! Art doesn't care how you feel!" he shouted, then released me. My foot caught on the TV power cord snaking across the floor, and I slammed hard into the tower of televisions, sending two sets crashing to the floor. The screen of the TV on top went black, and the tower caved in on itself with a terrible clamor.

Bess ran over to help me up, checking me for bruises. I was a little breathless, but otherwise unhurt.

It was lucky the TV screen hadn't shattered. I gathered myself to my full height, avoiding Sven's stony gaze. I wasn't particularly sorry about what had happened to his piece, and I didn't really want to apologize for the damage. After all, *he'd* thrown *me* into the installation.

"Sven, that was too much! Apologize to Nancy," Bess said, "or I won't help you with your performance."

He sighed deeply, and after a minute, he mumbled something that sounded like "sorry." Or maybe "sausage."

"Come on, everyone. Let's put the tower back together," said Bess. "Come *on*, Nancy."

If I didn't love my friend as much as I do, I would have rolled my eyes. But Bess had always been a peace-maker. She was happiest when everyone was getting along. So I bit my tongue and helped reassemble the TV pyramid. To defuse the tension, Bess asked Sven how he'd gotten interested in Duchess Strickland's art collection.

"After my senior year at River Heights High School, oh, five long years ago now, I took a summer art class. Mona Pearl Strickland, the Duchess's granddaughter, was in that class. She was already a prodigy. She could paint, she could sculpt, she could master any medium. Everyone said that was because she'd learned from the masters. She'd grown up copying the paintings in her grandmother's collection. Nobody else had access to art like that."

"I thought the Duchess and her family were estranged," I said.

"That was true. Mona Pearl's mom never came back to River Heights. During the school year, Mona Pearl lived with her mom in the city, but that year, she'd finally convinced her mom to let her spend a summer with her grandmother. My classmates thought Mona Pearl's grandmother was stuck-up. Everyone said the Duchess owned two paintings worth ten million each, but she never let anyone see them."

"Why not?"

"I think the Duchess was too greedy to share. I tried to get close to Mona Pearl, to work with her on a few projects, but she always said no. She told me she preferred to work alone. Stuck-up, just like her grandmother. But just like her grandmother, she was lying. . . ."

"Did you have a crush on Mona Pearl?" Bess asked.

"Certainly not! Mona Pearl was beautiful, yes, but if I had any interest in her, it was for her talent with a brush and her mastery of technique."

I rolled my eyes at that, but Sven went on.

"One day she invited me to the Strickland mansion for lunch in the garden. *That* was a fiasco! The Duchess and Mona Pearl were fighting about something or other. Mona Pearl could barely look at me, the finger sandwiches had *cilantro* in them, and even when I snuck away to snoop around the mansion, I could tell the Duchess didn't trust me. I looked everywhere for the Duchess's two precious paintings, but she must have hidden them. I started to think maybe my classmates were right. The Duchess was nothing but a stuck-up old hoarder."

"If she's so stuck-up, why did she just invite all of River Heights to her house for a party?" I interjected. Sven could talk all day if you didn't stop him. "She's putting on a show for us. You have to appreciate that. And I'm sure you'll get to see those priceless paintings if you come."

"She sure took her sweet time," said Sven. "The wealthy always do. I spent five years trying to track down a list of the pieces in the Duchess's collection. It's been impossible to find sales records. The only thing I know for sure is that the Duchess's secret paintings were painted by an artist called D. Shammas. Have you heard of him?" When I didn't answer, Sven gave me a dismissive wave. "Of course you haven't. I must assume the Duchess's Shammases have never been seen by anyone but the Duchess herself. Very little is known about the artist's life or work, and if she'd only share her paintings, we might learn a bit more about this reclusive genius. So you see, the Duchess's secrecy is a form of greed."

"But it's not true that no one else has seen the paintings you're talking about," I said slowly. "What about Mona Pearl? And the Duchess's daughter? And my dad? He said he had dinner at the mansion once, and he saw two small portraits of children hanging near the staircase. I'll bet anything those are the Shammases you're talking about."

Sven puffed out his chest like a pigeon as his speech grew more impassioned. "Don't you think it's vain for an old lady to call herself a duchess, especially when she has no connection to nobility? Of course I want the citizens of River Heights to see the Strickland collection, but the one-time event is still invitation only. Not exactly democratic! This is why the Duchess must be exposed!"

"And how do you propose to do that, Sven?" I asked. I looked over at Bess to see if she was buying into this melodrama. She was captivated.

Sven placed the last television at the top of the tower. His artwork was, once again, complete. "It would be foolish to pass up a performance. The mansion will be my stage. The guests, my unsuspecting audience. I will begin as the party reaches its height. There will be no announcement beforehand. There will be spectacle, truth, then revolution. I will stream the whole thing online. My message is for the people. But maybe gallery owners and critics will take note too."

"Well, that sounds . . . cryptic, and kind of rude. What if the Duchess is just trying to throw a nice party for everyone? Maybe she wants to apologize for going into hiding for so long. Couldn't you find some other, less obnoxious way to send your message?"

Bess put her hand on my arm. "Wait a second, Nancy. Sven is serious about his art. He's trying to send a message to society. His body is his instrument. That's how he tells the truth. And he asked me to help, so I'm going to perform too. It'll be fun! You have to trust me. Artsy people like bold statements. I don't think the Duchess will be upset."

"It's just not fair to steal the spotlight," I argued. "It's the Duchess's party, after all."

"Only a lapdog of the rich would defend the Duchess! She must hear the ugly truth!" shouted Sven, pirouetting around his TV tower.

Now Bess turned her placid blue gaze on Sven. "All right, Sven. I love your passion. I'm sure *our* performance will be a thing to remember. But promise me we won't start until late in the evening. That way, my friends and I will have plenty of time to enjoy the party."

Sven waggled his head oddly so I couldn't tell whether he meant yes or no, then ducked out the door.

"Come, slowpokes, come!" he called. "We wouldn't want to miss the Goddess Collective. Their 'performance' is about to begin." I could hear the quotation marks around "performance." It was clear Sven didn't think much of the Goddess Collective, whoever they were.

Bess and I hustled out of Sven's creepy studio. On our way out the door, I noticed a bulky tarp-covered object tucked away in a corner.

"What do you think's under there?" I asked. "A tower of typewriters? A pile of paper shredders? A fortress of fax machines?"

Bess giggled. "Who knows what's in that boy's weird mind."

We made our way down the warren of hallways and through an unmarked door that led into the annex of Slay Gallery. Everything was painted a blinding white—floor, walls, and ceiling—and recessed lights filled the rooms with a cold, bluish glow. I could hear the buzz of conversation and shuffling of feet around the corner. The main gallery was jammed full of visitors, all awaiting the inaugural performance at River Heights's first contemporary art gallery. I glanced at a few of the paintings as we hurried past. They were all portraits, ink on thick paper scrolls, and every face looked oddly familiar to me. One drawing looked just like the postal worker who always gave me a peppermint from the ceramic frog by her station. Another resembled my old orthodontist. And a third looked like—my dad? I didn't have time to stop for a closer look. In the main gallery, a bell was ringing.

It seemed like everyone in River Heights had turned out to see the Goddess Collective perform, along with a contingent of out-of-town visitors. If I stood on tiptoe, I could see a stage at the other end of the room, obscured by a pair of thick white curtains.

I spotted George in the crowd. As usual, her hair

was mussed and her shirt was wrinkled. She waved at us with both arms. Bess and I made a beeline for her while Sven duckwalked ahead of us, his hand stuck out, ready to shake.

"Hi, guys!" said George. "I see you brought the infamous Sven."

He frowned and pulled back his hand. "It is so exhausting, to be a legend among men."

George widened her eyes.

"I'm . . . sorry?"

"Your apology is unnecessary and unwanted," Sven said loftily before duckwalking away.

"Jeez," said George.

"He's just in a bad mood," Bess explained. "I don't think he's very good at watching other people succeed."

"Can't say I'll miss his company. When is this art happening getting started, anyway?" George asked.

"Should be any minute," I said.

Bess elbowed me in the ribs. "Cutie in a green cape, four o'clock," she whispered.

On the other side of the room, I spotted a tall black

boy in a grass-green wool cape leaning casually against the gallery wall, listening to Mr. Covarrubias, the high school art teacher. The boy scribbled something in a small black notebook, then caught us looking and winked. Bess gave him a little wave. The boy smiled.

The bell rang a second time, echoing against the gallery's high ceiling, signaling the beginning of the Goddess Collective's hotly anticipated performance. Four large men filed out in front of the curtains, holding wooden flutes up to their beards. The men tooted their flutes and stomped their feet out of rhythm. When this "music" came to a crescendo, two mysterious figures appeared on the stage in front of the men, wearing suits made of patches of multicolored faux fur that covered their bodies completely. One dancer wore a mask, but the other's face was visible. She had black hair and dark, shy eyes, and she danced, fluttering her hands.

"Diana Yip," said Sven in my ear.

"Thanks for the input," I whispered. "Next time you can tell me from over there."

The other dancer's masked face was further

obscured by a tall collar made of woven sticks that clacked and snapped as they shook their head. I was hypnotized by the soft swishing of fur and the sticks creaking in time with the couple's movements.

"Who do you think is under there?" George murmured, speaking my thoughts out loud.

I tried to determine the identity of the person under the mask, but it was impossible. The dancers moved like animals, like spirits, like whirling wind. Their energy was infectious. The whole crowd began to clap independently of the music. The masked dancer's collar rattled and clacked, and the sounds echoed in everyone's ears until we were dizzy and dancing too. Bess gave a whoop, and I saw Sven in the crowd doing the Macarena. Everyone shimmied and shook like wild things to the weird art music. It was a good feeling, half-silly, half-serious. Maybe that was how artists felt all the time. I thought maybe I'd been too hard on Sven. He was only an odd, silly, serious duck, and I could try to respect that, for Bess's sake anyway.

The flute players finished their song and filed

offstage. The dancers took a bow, and as they bent low, I managed to catch a glimpse of the crown of the masked dancer's head—curly black hair, parted in the middle—but was unable to take in more before whoever it was swept back up and held their arms wide to the crowd's applause.

This is what I love about being a detective, whether I'm on a case or not—discovering one small detail that tells a story. I imagined the dancer carefully combing and parting the hair that morning in front of the bathroom mirror, maybe taking a few extra minutes to smooth any stray strands, even knowing no one would see them. No one but me.

Diana Yip sat down on the stage, cross-legged, looking up at her partner. The masked dancer struck a warrior pose before the curtain and began to speak, their voice muffled and distorted through the layers of cloth and wood.

"Something terrible has happened to my grandmother. Early this morning, her home was burglarized. A priceless statue was stolen from her drawing room. No alarms were triggered, and the security cameras caught nothing. The thief escaped without a trace. No one will suspect her. And do you know why?"

Diana Yip said, "Tell them!"

"Because no one expects a child to steal from her own grandmother."

"Wait, who's her grandmother?" I wondered aloud.

"Her grandmother," whispered Sven, "is the Duchess of River Heights. That's Mona Pearl. The most talented student Mr. Covarrubias ever had. He said I was the second most talented. We'll see, Mona Pearl. Oh yes, we will."

The crowd rumbled; no one was sure how to react to Mona Pearl's introduction.

Sven pointed to an imposing blond woman in a silk turban and a Western-style suit with wide lapels embroidered in roses and thorns. "That woman over there is Angelica Velvet, the owner of Slay Gallery."

Angelica Velvet nodded and murmured something

to her black-turtlenecked assistant, who scurried away with two fingers pressed to her Bluetooth headset.

"Angelica is the one to impress," Sven went on. "If she likes what Mona Pearl and Diana Yip do next, she might give them their own show. But if she doesn't like it, well . . . they'll have to take their little act elsewhere."

Mona Pearl, still masked, grabbed the edge of one of the heavy white curtains; Diana Yip held the other. Through the collar, Mona Pearl proclaimed, "Ladies and gentlemen, for the first time, I can share with you the location of the missing statue of Diana, Roman goddess of the hunt. She is here with us, right now! When we are finished with her, she will be unrecognizable, an entirely new creation. Ladies and gentlemen, you are witness to the birth of a new muse."

Angelica Velvet raised a finely painted eyebrow so high it disappeared under her turban. Sven watched intently, eyes wide, twisting his long, thin fingers.

Diana said, "I, Diana Yip, hold the paintbrush."

Mona Pearl said, "I, Mona Pearl, hold the chisel."

Together, they chanted, "We are the Goddess Collective."

Mona Pearl and Diana Yip whisked open the curtains to reveal . . .

An empty pedestal.

CHAPTER THREE

Diana Disappears

THERE WAS A MOMENT OF STUNNED SILENCE before the dancers recovered their composure. "One moment, please," Mona Pearl told the crowd. "We're experiencing technical difficulties. Diana, stay here and keep talking. I'll see if it rolled away somewhere."

Diana stood nervously behind the microphone and blushed a darkening shade of pink. "H-how's everyone doing today?" she said in a tiny voice.

"Couldn't be better!" shouted Sven.

"Hush, Sven," said Bess.

Diana's blush deepened. Angelica Velvet frowned as another turtlenecked assistant shoved a phone screen in her face. Meanwhile, the masked dancer went rooting around behind the curtains and backstage. Finding nothing, she threw up her hands.

"Without a trace," she said in her muffled voice.

"Did you maybe hide it somewhere, as a surprise?" Diana asked.

Mona Pearl shook her collar. *No.* She kept shaking her head in rhythm, raising and lowering her hands in the air until it became a funny sort of dance.

This did nothing to settle the members of the crowd, who murmured to one another in increasingly concerned tones: When would the second act of Diana and Mona Pearl's performance begin? Had it already started? Was this all a part of the show? I wondered what was so special about that statue to be stolen twice in a single day.

"Wait a second . . . the pedestal's not empty," said Mona Pearl. "There's a piece of paper taped to the top. . . ."

"Don't joke," said Diana. She wasn't speaking into the microphone, but the gallery's high ceilings and echoing walls made it easy to overhear their conversation.

"No, really. Look!" Mona Pearl held up a small square of paper covered in blocky red letters. She handed the sheet to Diana, who read it silently.

I watched her face shift from embarrassment to anger.

"Read it to the crowd," Mona Pearl urged. "Maybe one of them wrote it."

"I don't want to," said Diana, crumpling the paper into a ball.

Mona Pearl grabbed the microphone. "It says, 'Fake Art.'" Her collar rattled like a rain stick. I could hear the laughter in her weird, muffled voice.

"Are you trying to make a joke? It's not funny." Diana's high-pitched voice rose even higher with indignation.

"I'm not," protested Mona Pearl. She jumped down from the stage and started dancing through the crowd, chanting, "Fake art, fake art, fake art," adding a sort of squat-and-spin movement as she checked under people's feet for signs of the missing statue. I could understand why Diana was upset. It didn't seem like Mona Pearl was taking the situation seriously.

"Without Diana, we're not a collective anymore," Mona Pearl was saying. "We're not goddesses, either. Nope! We're just a couple of humans! Sorry to disappoint you all!"

"Maybe you never wanted a collaborator!" Diana shouted, getting red in the face. "Is that what you're saying? Maybe this whole performance was just a bad idea. Maybe I'm better off alone!"

"Listen, Diana, I—" Mona Pearl pleaded.

"The Goddess Collective? Ha! I can't believe I fell for that name. You just made the performance all about you! All that work, all that planning, and for what? Just so you could humiliate me in front of everyone?"

"No, Diana! That's not true! We *are* a collective! I

value your opinion more than anyone else's! I—"

Mona Pearl started to say something else, but her words were muffled by the collar. Diana dissolved into tears and ran from the stage, pushing her way through the crowd to the exit.

Beside me, Sven snickered quietly to himself. I saw Angelica Velvet roll her eyes and turn her back to the stage.

Mona Pearl stood frozen, alone on the stage, for a long moment. Then she took hold of the microphone.

"Why doesn't she take off the mask?" I wondered.

"Maybe she feels more comfortable that way?" said Bess. "It is weird, though."

"Ladies and gentlemen, if you'd be so kind as to enjoy a brief intermission . . . I will go track down my collaborator. And my statue, too. I'm sure Slay Gallery will assist me in the search."

Angelica Velvet whirled around, unfurling one gold-taloned finger. "There will be no intermission! And no assistance," she bellowed. "That statue was Strickland family property, under Mona Pearl's exclusive guardianship. Slay Gallery cannot be held liable for its disappearance. Until the artists learn to execute their performance in a professional manner, Slay Gallery is closed."

Angelica turned to the assistant with the Bluetooth, who was hovering anxiously at her elbow. "Tawny, call the police. They can take it from here."

The masked dancer left the stage without fanfare. An unseen hand started turning off lights, driving the audience out into the sunset. I heard the wail of sirens pulling into the parking lot.

"Too bad those girls won't get the show they wanted," said Sven.

"Don't gloat, Sven," said Bess. "Let's just focus on making sure our performance goes off without a hitch."

"You're right, of course, goddess. I wouldn't want to be associated with such amateurish art. Come, let's go back to my studio and plan."

Bess asked George and me if we wanted to join

them. Personally, I'd had enough Sven for one day, plus I wasn't quite ready to leave the scene. George wasn't keen on spending more time with the obnoxious artist either.

"I'll meet you back at your house, Nancy," George said. "I heard Hannah's making lobster mac and cheese for dinner tonight in honor of Salvador Dalí."

"Ooh! Yum!" Bess exclaimed. She could never resist Hannah's cooking. "How do I get an invitation to the feast?"

"Fine, you can both join us," I said, "but I'd better make sure Hannah has enough for everyone."

"Don't worry, Nancy. I'll call your house. If Hannah needs anything, I can stop at the grocery store on my way over," George said, blowing us kisses.

I was curious what the River Heights PD would find in the way of clues, if they found anything. I decided to wait outside the gallery in hopes that my detective skills might come in handy. Through the gallery windows, I could see a pair of officers approaching Mona Pearl. The three of them exited the gallery and stood near the door. Mona Pearl was still wearing her mask. I decided I'd try to eavesdrop a little, just to see if there were any leads.

I leaned up against the wall outside the gallery, a little ways down from Mona Pearl and the police, and pretended to check my phone. Most of the audience had climbed into their cars and driven off, but I spotted Mr. Covarrubias in his parked car, talking on the phone, and the tall boy wearing the green cape hanging around at the edge of the parking lot, his gaze trained on the gallery doors.

The shorter of the two officers was a buff woman with a dark ponytail and a badge reading OFFICER GUTIERREZ. I overheard her saying, "So let me get this straight. The statue was stolen this morning from the Strickland mansion, but then it was stolen again?"

"That's right. I was the one who stole it the first time," Mona Pearl explained.

"And was your grandmother aware that you were taking the statue?"

"No. I was going to put it back after the performance."

"Why didn't you just ask her permission?"

"That's not important now," said Mona Pearl, her voice growing frustrated. "Now the statue really is missing."

"When did you last see it?" asked Officer Gutierrez.

"I carried it onstage before the performance. It must have been taken during the dance."

The officer made a note in her notebook.

"How do we know you didn't just steal the statue a second time?" asked the other officer, a sandy-haired man with the build of a college football player and a face like a golden retriever. His badge read OFFICER BURGERMUTT.

"Why would I steal from myself? Why would I sabotage my own performance?"

"Controversy? Attention? Stage fright? You tell me," said Officer Burgermutt. "Frankly, I think it's pretty suspicious you won't show us your face."

"Either way, we'll have to report this to Duchess Strickland," Officer Gutierrez added.

"Please, can't you look for a little while first?" Mona Pearl pleaded. "I'm sure the statue will turn up soon, and my grandmother doesn't need to know it was ever missing."

"Miss Strickland, when a valuable piece of artwork goes missing, that could be a serious crime. The statue's owner deserves to be informed of the investigation. I'm sure you and your grandmother can agree on that," said Officer Gutierrez.

"My grandmother and I don't see eye to eye."

"Hard to see eye to eye when you're wearing a mask all the time," muttered Officer Burgermutt.

"Can you think of any possible suspects?" Officer Gutierrez asked, ignoring her partner's comment. "Anyone who might want to sabotage your performance, or send a message to your grandmother?"

Mona Pearl shook her head and let out a wail. Officer Gutierrez tried to give her a comforting pat on the back, but the costume was too furry and prickly, and she quickly withdrew her hand.

"All right, we'll go back in and take a look around. Is there anything else we should know?"

"Just this," said Mona Pearl, thrusting out her palm. On it was the crumpled paper with the words *Fake Art* written in red ink.

"Weird ransom note," said Officer Burgermutt. "They didn't even ask for money."

He took the note with two fingers and held it up to the fading light to study it. Then he asked Mona Pearl to take him to the last place she'd seen the statue. She nodded and bowed theatrically, the collar dipping low enough to reveal the crown of her head again, with its neat middle part. Then she led Burgermutt through the gallery doors and out of my sight.

Officer Gutierrez hung back. She looked over at me.

"Hi, Nancy. Didn't know you were already on the case."

Officer Gutierrez had worked with my father on a few cases. Dad said she was one of the best investigators in River Heights. Apart from me, that is.

"I'm off the clock. I came to see the show. Just enjoying River Heights Art Week. I hope this doesn't mean the Duchess will cancel her party. Have you spoken to her already? I bet she called you in earlier today when her statue went missing the first time."

"Actually, no one contacted us from the Strickland mansion, and there weren't any alarms triggered. Mona Pearl must know the security codes."

"I thought the Duchess was estranged from her family."

"Breaking into your grandmother's house to steal a statue when you could've just asked—that sounds pretty estranged to me. Any idea what to make of this weird note? I know you have experience decoding cryptic messages."

"Well . . ." I thought about it. "It sounds like it was written by someone with strong ideas about art, but I couldn't say whether it's referring to the statue, Mona Pearl and Diana's whole performance, the opening of Slay Gallery, or something else entirely."

"Yeah, that's my hunch too, but good investigating means we need more than a hunch. So far, this note is our only evidence."

"Do you think the thief might strike again?" I asked in a low voice.

"Art thieves are an unusual type of criminal. They have to know a lot about the piece they're stealing and who might want to buy it. Otherwise, the stolen work is practically worthless," said Officer Gutierrez. "If it were me, I'd want to get the biggest bang for my buck. I don't think the thief will stop at just one statue."

"Hmm . . . seems to me like their best chance for a second theft would be during the Duchess's party, while everyone is distracted," I said.

"Exactly. Which is why I need to notify the Duchess ASAP. Excuse me, Nancy."

Officer Gutierrez dialed a number on her cell, put

the phone to her ear, and stepped through the gallery doors. I heard voices coming around the corner, a man and a woman, and it sounded like they were arguing. I reassumed my casual pose against the wall and pretended to be absorbed in my phone screen.

"The Duchess's party is already the talk of the town. A scandal will be the perfect way to make sure everyone shows up. No matter what happens at the party, we'll be talking about it for years," said the man's voice. It sounded like Sven.

The voices came closer and I heard Bess reply, her usually melodious voice now taut with frustration.

"How am I supposed to know how to act when I don't know what you're going to do next?"

"You have to trust me. Part two is the pièce de résistance."

The two of them turned the corner. "Oh, look. Nancy's still here," said Bess, coming over to me. Sven hung back, scowling. "Mind if I catch a ride home? I've had enough art for one day."

"Sure," I replied.

Sven gave Bess a curt nod and said, "Rehearsal tomorrow at three." He turned back toward the studio entrance without saying goodbye.

Bess sighed, half-dreamy, half-annoyed.

CHAPTER FOUR

Artsy Characters

WE MADE OUR WAY THROUGH THE PARKING lot toward my trusty blue hybrid. By this time, most everyone had left the gallery. The River Heights folks were probably heading home for dinner, while the city people went back to their bright lights and fancy restaurants. We passed a sleek gold convertible with a gigantic red rose airbrushed along the driver's side. I wondered who it belonged to. Maybe Angelica Velvet? Just beyond the convertible, I saw two people sitting on the hood of a beat-up red truck, their heads bent close in conversation. The setting sun was in my eyes, so I couldn't make out their faces. As we passed, I heard one of them say the word "Shammas." Sven had mentioned that name too.

Looking back over my shoulder, I could see the speaker's face: Diana Yip. She had changed out of her furry costume into a pair of paint-splattered overalls and a sweatshirt. Her eyes were red and puffy, but she wasn't crying anymore. Her companion was the young man in the green woolen cape—the one Bess thought was cute. I pulled Bess around to the other side of an old VW van nearby and held my finger to my lips.

"Ooh! Intrigue!" she exclaimed.

"Shh, I want to hear what they're saying."

Bess nodded. She and I were old pros at eavesdropping. It had come in handy in high school.

"Do you think the Shammas portraits will be safe?" I heard Diana say. She was speaking so softly, I had to strain to make out the words, but even from far off I could tell she was worried. "They haven't been seen in years."

"That's so like the Duchess. Keeping the best for herself," said the boy.

"Just like someone else we know," said Diana.

"I don't blame her for having secrets. It's in the Strickland DNA."

"Don't remind me. But on Saturday . . . anyone could just walk in and take what they want."

"Yes, that's the idea."

"What gave the Duchess the twisted idea for a party?"

"Madness and old age, I suppose," said the boy, examining his fingernails. "If you ask me—not that anyone ever does—there are better ways to be remembered. But the Duchess *was* always stubborn."

This conversation was setting off alarm bells in my head. It sounded like Diana and the boy in the cape were talking around something big. If I could find out what it was, maybe it would lead me to the missing statue.

"Excuse me. Hi," I said, stepping out from behind the van and pulling Bess up beside me. "Do you happen to know what time it is? My phone's dead and I don't want to be late for dinner."

"That's right, better head for home." The boy grinned. "You wouldn't want to get lost among the artists after dark."

"It's a quarter to six," said Diana Yip softly. She wouldn't make eye contact. Instead she stared fixedly at the screen of the tablet nestled in her lap.

"Thanks. I'm sorry about your performance," I said, thinking if I could get Diana to like me, she might say more about the mysterious Stricklands.

"Humph," Diana grumbled, scribbling something on her tablet with an index finger.

"Don't mind her," said the boy. He jumped down from the hood to stand beside us. "She'd rather draw than talk."

"How are you liking River Heights? You're a visitor, right? I don't think I've seen you around before. I'm Nancy."

"Hello, Nancy. I'm Zeke, painter and poet." He held out a hand for me to shake. I noticed the pads of his fingers were stained with ink, and there was pink paint under his fingernails. "Actually, I come from a long line of painters. They say painting died in the nineteenth century, but here I am, still living my life!"

"Are you going to the Strickland mansion next Saturday?"

"Yes, I am. And so is Diana, whether she likes it or not. She's nursing a broken heart. I think the Duchess's auction might be the cure she needs."

Auction? Maybe he'd misspoken. Or maybe he knew something I didn't.

"How well do you know the Duchess?" I asked.

"Not as well as I'd like," he replied, a faint smile playing around the corners of his mouth. "Nobody knows everything that's on that woman's mind. But enough about her. Who is this fine lady you brought with you? I saw you both in the gallery earlier."

I introduced Bess. She gave her best blushing, shy smile, the one that can melt a guy to a puddle.

"Is Diana your date to the party?" Bess asked Zeke.

Her voice fizzed with mischief. Bess isn't completely boy-crazy, but she never passes up a chance to flirt. As much as I hate to admit it, I actually felt a little sorry for Sven.

"We're going as friends," Zeke replied. "I'm here to support her in this difficult time."

Bess laid a hand on his arm. "You're too sweet. Did I hear you tell Nancy you're a poet? Would you write me a poem?" she asked, batting her eyelashes. Behind Zeke, I thought I heard Diana let out a derisive snort. But when I looked at her, she had her head bowed over the tablet, apparently absorbed in her drawing.

Zeke's brown eyes twinkled. "I will, but only if you promise never to read it."

Bess nodded. "I promise," she said solemnly, one hand over her heart.

Zeke took out his little black notebook and flipped to a blank page. I saw the book was overflowing with cramped, elegant script, some crossed through with thick slashes of black ink. What was he writing in there? I realized I'd never really thought about how poems were created. Did they come to Zeke fully formed, or did he write them over and over until he got the words right?

"Aren't you going to ask Bess what kind of poem she'd like?" I asked.

"A poem shouldn't be told what it is before it exists. Right now, her presence is all I need."

"Yes, my presence *is* that powerful. Thank you, Zeke," said Bess.

"Oh, brother," I said.

Zeke gazed into Bess's eyes for a long moment. I half expected him to kneel down and ask for permission to kiss her hand, like a medieval bard saluting his queen. Bess would make an excellent queen. She tilted her head, watching Zeke watch her.

In the absence of conversation, I heard the machinery beeping and grinding next door in the auto shop. A crisp spring breeze blew through my curls.

Zeke broke their gaze first. He took out a ballpoint pen, licked the tip, and began to write. Bess and I watched him for several minutes. He never paused, never crossed out, until he had covered an entire page top to bottom. I tried making out the words, but his oddly formal cursive was illegible to me. When he was finished, he tore the page from its binding, then crumpled it into a ball.

"Open your mouth, please," he said to Bess. I cocked an eyebrow.

Bess, delighted by the attention, stuck out her little pink tongue, as though to let Zeke check her tonsils. He nodded in satisfaction and placed the paper pill gently on her tongue.

"All right, swallow!"

Bess did as he asked without argument.

"What on earth did that have to do with poetry?" I said.

"Your stomach has eyes," Zeke said. "Listen, and your stomach will read what I wrote for you."

Bess nodded, beaming.

Diana, meanwhile, had put away her tablet and shimmied down from the hood of the car. She tapped Zeke on the shoulder and whispered something in his ear. A look passed between them, and then Zeke turned back to us. Diana unlocked the car and climbed into the driver's seat. She started the engine. Then, when Zeke still hadn't joined her, she gunned it once, twice, three times. The truck roared. Zeke laughed and waved her away.

"Hold your horses, girl. I'm coming!"

He turned back to us. "Nancy, Bess, it's time for us to part. You have dinner waiting, and I have my own business to take care of. Good to meet you both. You especially, Bess. See you at the Duchess's party." He bowed and swooped the wings of his green wool cape like a sorcerer, disappearing into the truck's cab. Diana pulled out of the spot at top speed and peeled out of the gallery parking lot, headed for the highway.

They'd left so quickly that I hadn't had time to ask Zeke what he'd meant about the Duchess's auction.

By the time Bess and I got back to my house, Hannah was already taking a huge tureen of mac and cheese out of the oven. The house smelled buttery and heavenly.

My dad and Ned hadn't arrived yet. Dad was probably making Ned comb through his legal books for one last crucial detail. He was a taskmaster, but that was what made him such an excellent lawyer. He never left anything to chance, preparing for every possible argument the opposing side might throw at him. Sometimes that meant he was late to dinner.

In the kitchen, George was slicing oranges for fruit salad under Hannah's watchful supervision. George couldn't always be trusted with pointy objects.

"So what did you hear, Nancy?" George asked. "Do the police have any leads?"

"Officer Gutierrez said there's not much to go on. And, worse, she thinks the thief won't stop at stealing one statue. The Duchess's party is the perfect opportunity for a major heist."

"Oh, goodness. The poor Duchess," Hannah fretted. "She must be distraught."

"Mona Pearl said her grandmother didn't know the statue was missing in the first place," I said.

"Why would she? There's so much art in that

house. One little old lady couldn't possibly keep track of it all," George said. "Do you have any suspects, Nancy?"

"It must have been someone there at the gallery. The statue went missing while Mona Pearl and Diana were dancing."

"So it wasn't Mona Pearl this time, then," George said.

"No, but that doesn't rule out the possibility that she had an accomplice. She stole the statue once already. It's the simplest explanation. Somehow, though, I don't think this case is simple."

"You haven't even told George about our new friend, Zeke," Bess said, a dreamy look on her face.

"Who's Zeke?" George asked.

"He's a poet and a painter," Bess answered breathlessly. "We met him in the parking lot. He wrote me a poem and made me swallow it."

"Wait, you *swallowed* a poem for this guy?"

"He's friends with Diana Yip. He's taking her to the Duchess's party."

"Sounds like you wish he was taking you instead," said George wryly.

"Don't get me wrong, I'm excited for my date with Sven. He's very artistic. I'm sure I'll learn a lot. And he's encouraging me to perform, too. This guy, Zeke, just had something special about him."

"He's much cuter than Sven, for one thing," I said.

"Who's cuter? I hope you're talking about me," came a voice from the doorway. Ned had finally been released from my dad's lawyerly clutches.

I skipped over to give him a kiss on the cheek.

"That's right. You're the cutest of them all," I said.

"Fee-fi-fo-fum. I smell lobster! Hi, Hannah. Hi, girls!" Dad entered the kitchen holding a heavy law book. Over the years, he'd perfected his ability to read while walking without tripping and falling on his face. He dropped the book on the kitchen table with a heavy thud. "I can't read one more line of this nonsense. Hannah, is there anything I can help with?"

"We're just about ready to eat. Would you set the table for me?"

"Of course," Dad replied, heading for the silverware drawer. "How was the performance, Nancy? Were you moved by the power of art?"

"More like the power of art theft," I said. "One of the Duchess's statues went missing in the middle of the show. If I were the Duchess, I'd be worried about the rest of my art collection. Do you think she's going to cancel her party?"

"No, I don't think so," my father said. "From what I recall, she's made of pretty strong stuff, and she doesn't change her mind once it's decided. Anyway, there are so many out-of-towners here for Art Week, I think they'd riot if the Duchess canceled. I can't say I know what these artsy characters are talking about half the time, but it's been really interesting having them around."

"That's a relief. Thanks, Mr. Drew," said Bess happily.

"Hmm, sure wish *I* could go to that party," Ned grumbled.

"Sorry, Ned. The trial starts a week from Monday and there's just too much to do." With that, my dad took the plates and silverware into the dining room. Ned glowered after him.

"Maybe the boss man will give me another break so you can at least show me your dress," said Ned, giving me a squeeze.

"I'll put in a good word for you," I said, patting his head. "But I guess that means I'm taking George as my date."

"Charmed, I'm sure," said George, grinning.

"Girls, can you help me carry these dishes into the dining room?" said Hannah.

"Of course!" I grabbed the tureen of mac and cheese. "I might just carry this up to my room and eat it all myself."

"Nancy Drew, you'd better not!" Hannah laughed. "Here, Ned, why don't you take this pitcher of iced tea? Be careful it doesn't spill!"

We proceeded into the dining room, set the dishes on the table, and took our seats.

"What do you think Zeke is doing right now?" Bess said dreamily.

"He said he had business to take care of," I replied. "I wonder what kind. . . ."

"Maybe we should've invited him to dinner."

"I'm sure we'll see him at the party. You can ask him then," said George. "By the way, Nancy, what time are you picking me up on Saturday? Remember, Mom won't let me drive. Not since the scooter incident."

George had briefly owned a motorized scooter. She'd managed to crash it within the first week, wiping out on the miniature golf course and damaging their plaster replica of an Egyptian sphinx. She ran right over the sphinx's left paw!

"I'll be there at six," I told her, spooning a big heap of macaroni onto my plate. "Make sure you wear something nice, okay?" I didn't mind driving us. I liked being able to take my friends wherever we needed to go. A good detective relies on herself, first and foremost, but a trusty mode of transportation is crucial.

It will be fun to go to a party with friends, I thought, *as long as George doesn't show up in hiking boots.*

And as long as the thief didn't return for the rest of the Duchess's art.

CHAPTER FIVE

A Glamorous Fraud

ON FRIDAY, THE DAY BEFORE THE DUCHESS'S party, I got a call from Bess.

"What are you wearing, Nancy? I was thinking maybe we should color-coordinate. Or get matching hats? I feel like this is the perfect occasion for fancy hats. What do you think?"

"I'm still tweaking my outfit," I told her, but that wasn't totally true. I couldn't even settle on a dress. I'd tried on everything in my closet, but nothing felt right. I couldn't figure out what the Duchess's invitation meant by "suitable dress." Did she expect formal gowns, or something avant-garde and artsy? Neither of those things were really my style. I decided to throw Bess off the scent the only way I knew how.

"I bet George is going to show up in jeans and flannel," I said.

"She *would*. I love her, but that girl was born without a lick of fashion sense."

"I'd better go over there and make sure she actually has something to wear. I'll call you later."

"Okay, good luck. I can't wait for tomorrow!"

When I got to the Faynes' house, I found George in her room, eyes trained on her laptop screen. With her rumpled T-shirt and short dark hair sticking up every which way, it looked like she hadn't logged off in days.

George was so absorbed in her screen that she didn't hear me enter the room. I snuck up behind her to see what she was working on. There were two versions of the same painted image blown up side by side on her screen—the head and upper body of a young woman dressed in blue. Her gown and hairstyle indicated that this painting was very old. Maybe European. But I couldn't see why George was scrutinizing the images so closely. They looked identical to me.

"Who's the lady?" I startled George so badly she nearly fell out of her chair.

"Nancy! I didn't see you!"

"Hi, sorry. I was just curious what you were working on. Isn't that the same woman in both portraits?"

"Yeah. Sort of." George zoomed in even closer on the image on the right. As she moused over the painted face, I noticed that in this version, the woman was wearing a large pearl earring and a pearl necklace, but the woman on the left was not. "The painting on the left is a genuine Vermeer, made in 1663. This one is fake. A really good fake, but still."

"Do you know who painted it?" I asked. I scooted in, trying to get as close to the screen as I could, looking for other inconsistencies. It was hard to tell. Even the brushstrokes seemed to match. There were just the two giveaways—that supersize pearl earring and the necklace.

George told me the counterfeit had been made in the 1930s by a Dutch painter named Han van Meegeren, who's now considered one of the most ingenious art forgers of all time.

"We learned about forgeries in art class a couple of years ago, and I got so curious I had to know more. Van Meegeren's copies of Vermeer fooled the Nazis!"

"That's crazy! How did he get away with it?"

"Van Meegeren always used old canvases and paints, just like Vermeer used. He even made his own brushes out of badger hair, because that's what Vermeer did. Every stroke is identical to Vermeer's style."

"That seems like a lot of work just to copy an artist's style or a painting."

"If you do it well, that forged painting might sell for millions of dollars. Plus, you get to fool everyone into thinking you're as good as an old master. That's the real payoff."

"Van Meegeren wouldn't get away with this today, would he?" I asked.

"Probably not. It's much harder to fool art buyers now. Scientists can use carbon dating and lasers and X-rays to discover hidden layers of paint and verify when the artwork was created."

"It's funny. Even though van Meegeren was obsessed with getting the brushstrokes right, he couldn't help but add some glamour of his own. That big honking earring. Why do you think he did that?"

George shrugged. "Maybe he wanted people to think his version was better. Maybe he wanted them to know *he* was the one who painted it, and not Vermeer."

"I guess that makes sense, in a twisted kind of way. You wouldn't want to show up somewhere fancy *without* your pearl earrings, would you?"

"I never wear earrings," said George, squinting at the screen.

"But you might, if you were, say, invited to a fancy party?"

"Mm, I'd probably just wear my nice jeans and a button-down shirt."

"Even if the invitation said 'suitable dress politely

requested' and you had a beautiful strawberry-blond date on your arm?"

"All right, all right. I think I see what you're getting at."

"Dad has Ned working all weekend, or I'd have asked him."

"You know, it's not exactly flattering to be your second choice." She shot me an annoyed look. "I clean up nice when I try. I just hardly ever try."

"Thank you, George!" I said, clapping with delight. "You'll have to rent a gown ASAP or there won't be any left in the shop."

"Ugh, I hate that formal-wear shop. It always smells like cats and my grandma's perfume. Plus, it's totally overpriced."

"This is serious, George! I really want to make a good impression."

"Okay, okay, I promise I'll dress up. I'm sure there's something 'suitable' in my closet. Why don't you help me pick out an outfit? Since you obviously want to."

"Don't mind if I do," I said, making a beeline for

George's overstuffed closet. "Maybe you can help me with something in exchange. When Bess and I went to visit Sven's studio, he told us that the Duchess has a pair of valuable works by someone called D. Shammas. I heard Zeke and Diana talking about them after the show too. You didn't learn anything about that artist in class, did you?"

"Nope. Never heard of Shammas. I can do some research, though."

"Yes, please."

George started typing at a frantic pace, opening tab after tab of Internet searches. She might not be so good at dressing up, but George Fayne was the only person I trusted to guide me through the Duchess's legendary art collection. I imagined Han van Meegeren, the forger, gluing delicate badger hairs onto his brush handle, and that reminded me of Mona Pearl, her face hidden behind the tall collar of carefully woven sticks. I liked the idea of a person who was totally dedicated to their art, even if no one else understood what they were doing.

Ever since that day at Slay Gallery, I couldn't stop thinking about Mona Pearl's missing statue. She'd said the statue depicted Diana, the Roman goddess of the hunt. I wondered if that was significant. How could a goddess vanish from a packed gallery? And who would want to steal from the Duchess's grand-daughter?

In order to investigate the missing statue, I'd need to blend in among the Duchess's guests. I wanted to look fabulous enough that any of these artsy people would feel comfortable talking to me, maybe even comfortable enough to let something slip.

George's closet seemed to be filled with nothing but lumpy sweaters and hanger after hanger of wrinkled button-down shirts printed with zigzags, polka dots, birds, palm trees, lightning bolts, and bicycles. Finally, all the way at the back, I found a single sleeveless blue dress with its tags still on. I wrestled it out and held it up for George to see.

"What about this? If you added a belt and some heels, it would be adorable."

George glanced over and wrinkled her nose.

"I'll . . . think about it. Nancy, how do you spell 'Shammas'?"

"S-H-A-M-M-A-S, I think. Why?"

"It's just, when I search that name, the only things that comes up are some accountant in Illinois and a company that makes dust mops."

"Try 'D. Shammas' plus 'paintings' plus 'millions.' Sven said he isn't well known, but his work is very valuable."

George hit search.

I crossed the room to peer over her shoulder. *Zero results.* That was weird. Maybe we weren't spelling it right. Or maybe there were things only artistic types knew about, and D. Shammas was one of them.

"Enough distractions. If you're not going to wear that dress, what are you going to wear?"

"Don't worry. I have a plan."

"Care to share it?"

"I think you're going to be very surprised," George said with a devilish grin.

By the time I got home, I was almost frantic. The party was tomorrow and I still didn't know what to wear. Without the right dress, it would be totally obvious that I was just some local teenager, trying to soak up a little of the Duchess's glamour. *Maybe I should just go naked,* I thought. *I'll say I'm doing it for my art.* Then I realized Sven would probably do something exactly like that for his disruptive "performance." Bess would show up in some stunning gown she'd made herself. I could never outshine her. I'd have to think of something different, and fast. I stomped indoors and kicked off my shoes, making a racket.

"Nancy, is that you?"

Hannah was in the kitchen, bifocals perched on the tip of her nose, threading a long, curved needle with pomegranate-colored thread. Balanced on her knees was a hatmaker's mannequin with a small puff of pink netting secured at its crown by straight pins.

Hannah had laid out a whole array of decorations

on the kitchen table: lengths of embroidered trim, flowers made from paper and scraps of fabric, curls of felt, beads, ribbons, feathers, and a pair of glossy, artificial cherries. I couldn't help reaching out to stroke the petal of a silk magnolia near her elbow.

"Hi, Hannah," I said, unable to hide the unhappiness in my voice. It was no use trying, anyway. Hannah always knew how I was feeling.

"What's wrong, Nancy?"

"It's such a dumb thing to be upset about. But I can't decide what to wear to the Duchess's party, and I'm almost out of time!"

"You always look lovely, no matter what you wear," she said, beaming at me. "A party should be a time to celebrate. Wear what feels good. I'm making myself a nice hat, see?"

"I didn't know you could make hats!"

"I'm a woman with hidden talents." Hannah laughed. "When I was young, I enrolled in a one-year millinery school. I thought I would open up a little shop. But you never know what life will throw at you.

My mother was ill, so I came home to take care of her. My little shop never came to be."

"Wow, Hannah, I had no idea."

"It's all right, Nancy. Mainly I'm just a fan. I watch the Royal Ascot and the Kentucky Derby every year. I love seeing all the latest styles. I make the occasional hat when I have the time, even though it's only for my own enjoyment."

"So the Duchess's party will be your fashion debut?"

"That's true," Hannah replied. "Oh goodness, that makes me a little nervous."

I looked at the hat in progress and tried to picture Hannah wearing it. The puffy shape harmonized with Hannah's round, kind face, and the soft pink tulle set off her eyes. It was perfectly designed, especially for her.

"You have nothing to worry about. In that hat, you'll turn everyone's head. How do you decide what to make? How do you choose the colors or which decorations to use?"

"It's hard to explain. . . . I guess I just go with what

feels right. If it makes me happy, I'll use it. Same as cooking. If it tastes good to me, I know you'll probably like it too."

"I think I see what you're saying. . . . You make hats about who *you* are, not about what other people want."

Hannah nodded. "Precisely. Now, what do you think about these cherries?" She dangled the red globes in front of my nose.

"Definitely add those."

"That's what I wanted to hear. The next question is how to attach them. . . ."

I closed my eyes, and suddenly I could picture it: my suitable outfit, the one I'd wear to the Duchess's party to make everyone who saw me think, *There's Nancy Drew, the best detective in River Heights. Isn't she fabulous!*

"I think I finally know what I want to wear," I said, "but I'll need to borrow your sewing machine. And maybe one of these silk flowers. Pretty please?"

Hannah waved an agreeable hand in my direction,

already absorbed in her creative process. Breathless with excitement, I ran to the hall cabinet where Hannah kept the sewing machine, hauled it out by the handle, and lugged it upstairs to my room. I switched on my bedside lamp. I'd have to stay up late, but it would be worth it for a dress that suited *me*.

CHAPTER SIX

Arriving in Style

IT WAS AFTER FIVE O'CLOCK ON SATURDAY by the time I finished the last adjustments to my party dress. The invitation said the celebration would start at six, and I still had to pick up Bess and George. I stepped into my dress and zipped myself in, pleased by the perfect fit.

Then I phoned Bess and George on a three-way call, putting them on speaker while I curled the ends of my hair.

"Are you both ready to go? Can you wait outside for me? I'm running a tiny bit late!"

"I await my chariot," said George.

"Don't worry about me, Nancy, I'm getting a ride with Sven," Bess said.

"On his art cycle? You've got to be kidding."

"Don't listen to her, Nancy. It's an imposter! The Bess I know would never set foot on something called an 'art cycle'!"

"Shut up, George," said Bess.

"Love you, Cousin."

"Promise me you'll wear a helmet," I said to Bess.

"And squash my hair? You're dreaming, Drew."

"Now *that* sounds like the real Bess," said George.

"Bess, I'm not joking! Motorcycles are dangerous. Especially when driven by eccentric artists who don't know how to walk like a normal person!"

"Fine, fine. I'll wear the stupid helmet. But you're signing on to fix my hair when I get to the party."

"Deal. See you there!"

"Can't wait to see your dress!" Bess squealed.

"Me neither," said George.

"I'm hanging up! I have to finish getting ready.

George, I'll be there in fifteen minutes!"

"Roger that," said George. I ended the call.

Standing in front of my mirror, I admired my handiwork. My dress was velvet with a blue skirt shaped like a bell, where I'd hidden not two, but four pockets for gathering clues. I'd taken two of my dad's old coats and cut them up, then sewed the pieces back together to create a reconstructed trench coat that belted at the waist. I touched up my hair and added a little blush, then nodded at my reflection. Holding out a white-gloved hand, I said, "Nancy Drew, detective. And you are? Charmed. Charmed, I'm sure."

I jumped as Hannah politely rapped on my doorframe. "Oof, this is embarrassing." I groaned.

"Don't worry. I was doing the same thing fifteen minutes ago," she said, chuckling. "But we'd better go now, or we'll be late!"

Hannah pulled out a bundle of glittery netting from her coat. It was her finished hat, a pink fascinator decorated with the plastic cherries and small loops of sequins. She affixed it to her head at a jaunty angle.

I clapped with delight. "That hat is awesome, Hannah. You're so elegant, like a duchess!"

Hannah hugged me, nearly crushing her hat in the process.

Just then my dad and Ned emerged from the study, Ned rubbing his eyes blearily. When he saw me, his jaw dropped open.

"Nancy, is that you? Of course it is. That's the most Nancy Drew outfit I've ever seen. You look incredible."

"Yes, it suits you perfectly," my dad chimed in. "But . . . are those my trench coats?"

"Not anymore," I said. "Anyway, you hadn't worn these in years."

"You certainly look better in them than I ever did."

"Thanks, Dad. Any chance you might release my boyfriend from your study dungeon so he can escort your beautiful daughter to the party?"

"I'm afraid not. At this rate, we'll be working through the night."

Ned groaned. "Need more coffee . . ."

"I brewed a fresh pot, extra strong," said Hannah. "That should keep you going until sunrise."

"Thanks, Hannah. I don't know what we'd do without you," my dad replied.

"We'd better leave now. My date is probably wondering where we are . . . ," I said.

Ned groaned louder. I gave him a kiss on the cheek as a consolation prize and waved goodbye to my dad.

"Be good, boys!" I shouted over my shoulder, swirling my skirts around me like Cinderella.

Hannah and I got into the hybrid and headed for George's house. When we pulled into the Faynes' driveway, I spotted a stranger leaning in the doorway. The person wore a navy-blue tailored tuxedo with a gold stripe up the leg and held a bouquet of pink roses. I wondered if George's parents had invited a friend to drive to the Duchess's with them, or if this was their chauffeur. The stranger's hair was slicked back, so it took me a moment to recognize that this dapper person was really my dear friend George Fayne.

George strode down the driveway, holding the roses to her chest. I noticed she was wearing a bow tie patterned with golden diamonds, with a matching pocket square that perfectly complemented my dress.

"Holy cow," I said. "How did she know what colors I was wearing?"

Hannah giggled at my stunned expression. "A little birdie told her."

"You?"

"Guilty as charged," Hannah replied. "She wanted to set off your dress."

George sauntered over to the driver's-side window, propped her elbows on the glass, and gazed into the car with a mischievous spark in her brown eyes. On her lapel was a gold pin in the shape of a bow and arrow.

"In memory of the Duchess's lost goddess statue," she said, pointing to the pin, before solemnly offering me the bouquet through the window.

I accepted it, but I was still too stunned to say thank you.

"Hello to you, too, Nancy. Do you like my gown?"

"So handsome," said Hannah. Her voice trembled a little, so I knew she was barely holding back laughter.

"Thanks. The tux is vintage. My dad wore it to his senior prom. He can't even button the jacket anymore, but it fits me perfectly."

George climbed into the back seat and stretched out like a cat.

"I like your hat, Hannah. And Nancy's hair."

Hannah finally let her giggles out. "Wait until you see her dress! She even added secret pockets."

"Oh, so did I!" George exclaimed. "Great minds, Nance. Look! I have three inside the jacket. One for my blue fingerprint light, one for my magnifying glass and sketchbook, and one more for my phone . . . Oh, and I'm wearing the waterproof smart watch I got for Christmas. It records audio and video, and it'll even take a picture if I press this button here." She pushed her wrist between the front seats to demonstrate.

"She thinks she's James Bond now," I said, but I was touched by the trouble George had taken with her appearance. This was as sharp and put-together as I had ever seen her. And she did look a little like James Bond.

We passed the drive trading theories about who would show up to the Duchess's party. Hannah thought we might see a few local celebrities, and maybe even a movie star or two. George had a feeling the guest list might be more eclectic, with local schoolteachers and butchers and pharmacists and accountants rubbing elbows with eccentric artists and wealthy collectors.

I kept thinking about Zeke's slip of the tongue. Could it really be true that the Duchess was selling off her art? All those beautiful works of art would leave River Heights forever. I'd better make sure I got a good look at those famous Shammases tonight. It might be my last chance to see them here in River Heights.

A police car was parked at the gates of the Strickland estate. Chief McGinnis was sitting on the hood dressed in a tuxedo, trying to tie his bow tie.

I rolled down my window.

"Hi, Chief McGinnis. What are you doing here?"

"Attending the Duchess's party, same as you. I have the night off. Now if I could just get this darn bow tie to stay put . . ."

"Come around to this side, Chief," said Hannah. "I can tame it."

"Bless you!" he said. "Last time I wore one of these neck-stranglers was at my brother's wedding ten years ago."

Hannah tied the bow tie in a perfect knot and straightened Chief McGinnis's collar.

"There you go. Neat as a pin."

"Thanks, Hannah. Save a dance for me, will you?"

"I'd be delighted."

We joined a line of cars creeping up the Strickland estate's long gravel drive. The road looped through a corridor of cottonwood trees, around stone-edged garden beds and terraced lawns filled with topiaries and fountains that made strange shapes in the falling dark. At the end of it all, the Strickland mansion loomed like a gigantic vanilla cake. The three-story structure was built of a white stone that glowed softly in the twilight. Its tall windows commanded a sweeping view of the grounds and arriving guests. The door and window frames were painted carmine red, and I spotted two stone dogs stationed on either side of the front door. Pillared verandas extended to the east and west of the grand entrance, where red-jacketed valets were busy parking and directing guests.

As we waited, we watched the other guests exit their vehicles in eye-popping outfits. A tall man with long, lustrous hair and a waxed mustache hurried up the steps to catch his friends, hoisting the lavender skirts of his silk kimono. A group of four women in sequined coveralls and enormous platform shoes walked in synchronized motion, leaning on one another for support. I saw a man with a full set of antlers on his head, decorated with roses and draped in shimmery fabric. George pointed out another woman with orange hair in a bizarre dress that looked like it was made of twisting black snakes. One chestnut-haired woman in a loud orange, pink, and green caftan wore enormous golden discs in her ears, so heavy that her earlobes nearly touched her shoulders.

I saw a few familiar faces mixed in among the artier guests. There was Maria the librarian in a smart three-piece suit, the director of the fine arts museum, Eric Hovnanian, and his husband, Carl, in matching plum smoking jackets, Joe Archer from the new arts complex, and even my old high school art teacher, Mr. Covarrubias, with his silver hair tied back in a neat ponytail and his paint-stained fingers scrubbed clean.

Finally it was our turn at the valet stand. After I handed my keys to the attendant, he pointed us toward another long line forming outside the mansion's front entrance.

"Go on ahead through the security checkpoint," he said.

Security checkpoint? The Duchess really wasn't taking any chances. I assumed she had a state-of-the-art surveillance system guarding her treasures inside, but that hadn't been enough to protect her Diana statue.

George stopped me before we reached the entrance.

"I want a good look at this outfit, Nance. Could you give me a spin?" I obliged. George applauded, beaming. "Wow, can't believe I'm going to a party with this high-fashion detective. Someone should paint you," she said.

George was right. I had been so nervous about fitting in with the arty types and their grand fashions, but now I was the one turning heads. The man with the antlers stopped in his tracks to get a better look.

"Honey, that coat is to die for. Is it Ralph Lauren?" he asked.

"Nope. It's Nancy Drew couture," said George proudly.

The man dipped his antlers in deference, then floated away.

More red-jacketed staff directed us past the imposing double doors, where we joined a line of guests waiting to go through a metal detector. The Duchess had hired private security for the evening, but I also noticed quite a few River Heights police officers among the guests. Bad news for the statue thief. They'd have to be crazy to try something tonight, but then again, I also knew there was a certain class of criminal who would consider this impossible heist an exciting challenge.

Ahead of us, the woman with the heavy gold earrings was passing through the metal detector with a creamy brown coat folded over one arm. The machine lit up with flashing red alarms. A security guard asked her to please remove her earrings. I could hear her shouting from the back of the line.

"But these are twenty-four-karat gold!"

The guard asked the woman to empty her purse and remove her shoes and go through the gate again, but the alarm sounded a second time.

"I'm afraid it has to be the earrings, ma'am."

"This is an outrage! An encroachment on my civil rights! These earrings are genuine. I won't be insulted by a *machine*! Why, I ought to have you sued within an inch of your life!"

I felt a tap on my shoulder and turned to find Beverly DeSantos standing behind me. Bess, George, and I had met her when we were investigating a case in Shady Oaks involving her famous grandfather's photographs. Tonight, her dark curtain of hair was twisted with gold and silver threads.

"It's good to see you here, Nancy," Beverly said. "A party like this always attracts some peculiar types. I assume you already know that woman in the caftan. Angelica Velvet, the owner of Slay Gallery."

"Wow, I didn't recognize her."

"Yeah, wasn't she blond before?" said George.

"I think so. . . . She looks totally different from last week at the gallery opening."

"That's her style. Angelica's always trying out different looks. She has a whole room in her house just for wigs," said Beverly.

"That's an expensive habit."

"Angelica has always been about her profits. Did

you know she's currently being investigated for the sale of a forged painting? It's why she had to leave the city and come to River Heights. Or at least, that's the art world gossip."

We watched Angelica Velvet yank the earrings from her ears and throw them to the ground before marching through the detector for a third time. No alarms.

"Everything about her is fake, down to the earrings." Beverly gave a bitter laugh.

"Don't worry," I said. "I'll keep an eye on Ms. Velvet tonight in case she decides to try and smuggle something out under that caftan."

It was George's turn to walk through the detector. Something in her tuxedo tripped the alarm, and the security guards took her aside and passed a wand over her jacket until they discovered a small pocketknife tucked away in one of her jacket's hidden pockets.

"I don't intend to use it! It's only in case of emergency," George protested. "You see, my date has a tendency to get into scrapes."

"This is a *party*," said one of the guards, an older man with a walrus mustache. "There won't be any emergencies. You'll just have to make sure your date stays out of trouble."

"It's okay, George. I don't think we have anything to worry about," I said, half trying to convince myself. At this very moment, the statue thief might be waiting in line right behind us. I'd have to keep my eyes peeled for anyone suspicious, though in this crowd of avant-garde fashionistas, that seemed like an impossible challenge.

"You can pick up your knife at coat check when you leave," the guard said, dismissing us.

Just inside the entrance was a small foyer with a coat-check station on the left. Angelica Velvet was speaking sharply to the coat-check boy, shaking her cappuccino-colored coat in his face.

"I expect my coat to still be spotless when I return. It's made from vicuña wool, which is exceedingly rare and delicate. My coat is probably worth more than your parents' whole house. Don't touch it, don't look at it, don't even breathe on it, or I will know."

The coat-check boy nodded, absolutely terrified. He took the coat with two fingers and settled it onto a wooden hanger. Given the incident with Angelica's "twenty-four-karat-gold" earrings, I was skeptical of her claims about the coat.

I told George and Hannah I'd catch up with them inside. As Angelica turned away, her upper lip curled in disgust at the coat-check boy's ignorance, I walked right up and introduced myself. "Angelica Velvet? My name is Nancy Drew. I was at your gallery opening last week."

Angelica looked down her long, horsey nose and tossed her chestnut-brown wig.

"Interesting coat, little girl. Is it vintage?"

"In a way, I guess it is. I made it from two of my dad's old coats."

"Hmm. It's certainly . . . unusual."

"Thank you," I said sweetly, choosing to take that as a compliment. "I really enjoyed Diana Yip and Mona Pearl's performance. It's too bad that we never got to see the second half. I think a lot of people in River Heights would've liked to see what they did next. Do you have any idea what happened to Mona Pearl's statue?"

"The police tell me they are investigating." Angelica sniffed. "But I must say, as a business owner, it is of serious concern when the artists I invest in can't manage to keep track of their own work. My opening was ruined!"

"It's not Mona Pearl's fault that someone decided to steal her statue," I said. "It's important to learn who did, though. The thief could strike again at any moment. If the heists continue, River Heights's arts revival might be over before it begins. Wouldn't that be awful?"

Angelica Velvet waved a hand in my face. "Don't fool yourself, child," she scoffed. "River Heights was never going to be the next arts destination. I only opened my gallery here because Duchess Strickland gave me the building practically for free. It was Duke's factory once, when he was selling cat toys."

"Interesting. Do you think the person who stole the statue from your gallery knew it belonged to the Duchess?"

"It's likely, I'm sure, given our long business arrangement. Duchess Strickland was my first-ever client. I've sold every piece she's ever brought to market. Or, at least, I used to. We haven't spoken in years, and even when we were on good terms, she never so much as invited me for tea at the mansion! At least, not until now, along with everyone else in this backwater town."

"But she gave you that building for your gallery. Doesn't that show she's at least a little bit grateful?"

"I'm doing a public service, really, bringing cutting-edge artists to this soulless suburb. The question is whether your fellow normals can learn to appreciate my taste."

Angelica's cold blue eyes kept scanning the room, looking for more important people to talk to. I could tell she was growing irritated with me, but I had to ask one last question.

"Artists like Diana Yip and Mona Pearl don't come around every day. Don't you think they deserve another chance to perform?"

"I can't work up much sympathy for Miss Pearl. I gave her a shot as a favor to her grandmother. But what I saw didn't impress me. Without the statue, those girls are nothing but a couple of edgy ballerinas. No, a woman of my fine taste is interested only in visionary, original art. Tonight there's only one artist I'm interested in. D. Shammas, creator of the jewels of the Duchess's collection. I'd like to know where she's keeping those portraits. . . ." Angelica craned her neck, trying to see beyond the foyer to the artistic treasures of the Strickland mansion's inner galleries.

"Are you absolutely sure you don't know what happened to that statue? I'm sorry to keep asking, but I'm just so curious. Maybe it was simply misplaced by one of your gallery staff—"

"I refuse to answer such an insulting question."

Angelica Velvet stormed off, her caftan billowing

behind her like an angry wind. I handed my decon-structed jacket to the coat-check boy. What Angelica had said made me think. Angelica Velvet would want to ensure there was lots of buzz around her new business because buzz brought in customers. So maybe a failed gallery opening was even better than a successful one. But would Angelica Velvet steal from her benefactor just for the attention?

If what Beverly had heard was true and Angelica *was* selling forged paintings, that made her someone worth keeping my eye on. She knew something about that missing statue. I was sure of it. Maybe the possibility of extra publicity around her gallery might be enough to convince her to make the statue disappear. . . .

CHAPTER SEVEN

The Blank Wall

GATHERING MY SKIRTS, I HALF WALKED, half skipped through the marble foyer, past two stern suits of armor and a row of potted topiaries, into the main hallway, which doubled as an enormous gallery. The Duchess's red-jacketed staff flitted through the crowd with trays of hors d'oeuvres and flutes of sparkling water on silver platters. More guests streamed in behind me, and the flow of the crowd carried me along the impossibly high-ceilinged hallway, past a marble staircase, and into a grand ballroom.

Everywhere I looked, the walls were cluttered

with painting after painting in various styles, and they seemed to be arranged by historical era: first came gold-painted religious icons inscribed with Cyrillic letters and African masks carved from dark wood, then neat geometrical compositions of Greek philosophers in the forum and Islamic scientists in turbans making measurements with sextants and compasses, then courtly scenes of noblewomen in furs, foggy Japanese mountaintops done in ink washes, and ceremonial cloths printed with intricate patterns. Off to my right was a grand marble staircase flanked by gigantic marble urns stuffed with white roses, and two carved benches with red velvet cushions. George and Hannah were sitting on the bench to the left of the staircase, gazing up at the white marble wall.

I snuck up behind them and leaned very close to George's ear. She didn't notice me. They were both totally engrossed in looking at the perfectly blank wall ahead of them. George's brow furrowed the way it did when she was thinking hard about something.

"Whatcha looking at?" I said in my goofiest voice.

George jumped to her feet. Hannah let out a little "Oh!" of surprise.

"Jeez, Nancy, are you trying to give us heart attacks? We're just trying to have a quiet moment in the presence of great art over here."

"Uh . . . am I missing something? You two are looking at an empty wall, right?"

"It's empty now, yes. But I don't think that's always true," said George. "I mean, why else would the Duchess have these two benches here? They're turned to face . . . something."

"Whatever usually hangs here must be the Duchess's favorite paintings," said Hannah. "I don't see anything else with its own bench. She probably sits here all the time, just looking at them."

Suddenly I remembered my conversation with Dad about his visit to the Strickland mansion. He'd said the two portraits he was so obsessed with hung next to the Duchess's staircase. Was that what was missing? Why would the Duchess remove them, especially when she had invited everyone to her house for a celebration of art? Hiding paintings wasn't very celebratory.

"Don't you think it would get boring looking at the same old paintings day after day?" asked George.

"Not necessarily," said Hannah. "Life changes us. It changes the way we see."

"In my experience, when a painting changes or moves, it's usually because there's someone hiding behind it," I replied. "And besides, if all art changed over time, how would we ever know what an artist was trying to say?"

"I think art is meant to tell you more about yourself than about the person who made it. But I'm no expert," Hannah replied.

"My art history teacher used to tell us, 'Art evokes the mystery without which the world would not exist,'" George said. "I thought you'd like that, Nancy. It's a quote from the painter René Magritte. He was a surrealist, so you know he was a little wacky. But this is all theoretical, anyway. There aren't any actual paintings for us to look at *or* get bored of."

"That's true. I wonder why . . . ," I mused.

Just then we heard people behind us oohing and aahing. I stood and turned just in time to see the crowd parting to make way for a beautiful girl in a shimmering cream-colored gown, her hair twirled up away from her neck and crowned with a futuristic tiara. The girl smiled and waved to her admirers as though she'd been doing it all her life. It took me a moment to realize that the shimmering girl gliding toward us was Bess.

"Cousin, is that you?" George asked in amazement.

"Cousin, is *that* you?" Bess said, gesturing to George's spiffy duds.

"Bess, you look like a space princess!" I exclaimed.

"Thank you very much, Nancy!" Bess said. "I had to steam the skirt in the bathroom after that awful ride on Sven's art cycle. He made me sit on a dirty old tarp because he insisted on keeping the bike covered. He claims he's waiting for the right moment to reveal his art."

"Where is Sven, anyway?" I asked.

"He's preparing for his performance," said Bess,

trying to sound supportive, but unable to keep a note of exasperation from her voice. "He told me he has to meditate in absolute silence. I'm supposed to meet him outside just before the Duchess's speech. He barely looked at my outfit. I made it myself. The tiara is papier-mâché."

"Bess, it's amazing. If he can't see that, then he's not worth your time," I said.

"Hear, hear!" said George. "Now, let's go see what fancy snacks the Duchess cooked up for us."

"Finally, someone with sense." Bess giggled. "I can't believe you didn't even *try* to wear a dress. But I have to admit the tux is pretty awesome."

"I had to look nice to impress my date!" said George. "I wouldn't dress up for just anybody."

"That's mighty sweet of you, George," I said, fluttering my eyelashes like a Southern belle.

Bess, George, Hannah, and I made our way past the staircase into the ballroom, arm in arm. The room was cavernous, with a wooden parquet floor and a huge stone fireplace at each end, but with all the guests chatting and eating delicate canapés, it felt almost full. The walls here were full of paintings in heavy gold frames. The high domed ceiling was painted a cerulean blue, with the constellations picked out in gold leaf. A single, enormous crystal chandelier descended from the center of the dome to illuminate the room. The chandelier swayed slightly in an invisible breeze, its cut-glass jewels tinkling.

Near the dessert table, I spotted Riley, a photographer I'd also met in Shady Oaks. She grinned and snapped a shot of me striking my best superstar pose while George and Bess attacked a tower of pretty iced tea cakes. Abby Heyworth, co-owner of Black Creek Farm, floated over to greet them. Her gown looked like it was made of old burlap sacks and bits of grass. "It's fully compostable!" Abby exclaimed. I watched George and Bess paste on polite smiles, but I knew they were trying not to burst into laughter. Hannah drifted away from us to chat with Mr. Covarrubias and Judge Nguyen.

Bess grabbed my arm and pointed to a green-cloaked shape on the far side of the room.

"Look, there's Zeke! I have to tell him I had a dream about his poem. I know exactly what he wrote!"

I was glad my friend had already bounced back from her disappointing date. She's always so good at seeing the best side of a person. I think it's what makes her so prone to crushes.

I noticed Diana Yip standing near Zeke, drawing on her tablet. Zeke said something to her, and in reply, Diana shook her head, never looking up from the screen. Her shoulders were hunched and her hair hid her face. Her whole body looked sad. The bizarre dress she had on looked like it was made of thousands of bird's beaks, which did nothing to brighten up her appearance.

That missing statue was a wedge between Mona Pearl and Diana, and anyone could see Diana was miserable without her friend. There was no sign of Mona Pearl anywhere. She had to have been invited—she was family. But since I didn't actually know what Mona Pearl looked like without her mask, she could have walked right past me and I wouldn't have known. I stood on tiptoe and conducted a quick scan of the ballroom, looking for the one detail I knew about Mona Pearl—her black hair was parted down the middle. I saw lots of colorful hair, braided and coiled, slicked back or puffed out or twisted into tight curls and topped with jeweled pins, veils, hats, and flower crowns. Nowhere did I see a middle part as straight as Mona's.

I was thinking of ways to get closer to Zeke and Diana when I saw a hand waving from the other side of the room. Susan, the curator from the Carlisle Historical Museum, was standing with a pretentious-looking man I didn't know.

"Nancy Drew! Come and say hello!" Susan called.

As I crossed the room, I noticed that Angelica Velvet had marched over to speak with Zeke and Diana. Her fake gold earrings swung aggressively. From her stabbing hand gestures, I guessed the gallery owner was angry about something, and she expected Zeke to answer for it. She extended one talonlike fingernail and poked him in the chest. What was *that* about? I made a mental note to ask Zeke when I got the chance. But first I had to say hello to Susan and make small talk with her rather rude-looking companion.

The pair was standing beside a platform, on top of which an imposing granite throne was positioned. The throne had a striped marble seat, high carved armrests topped with stone pommels, and ivy carved around the base. I wondered if the Duchess actually sat in that throne and ordered people around, like a real duchess might.

Susan's acquaintance had a solemn frown on his distinguished face. He wore a gray turtleneck and a sharkskin jacket, a red baseball cap turned backward, and a silver necklace made to look like barbed wire. I saw that his fingers were loaded with heavy gold rings.

"So good to see you, Nancy," she said, giving me a hug. "This is Rufus Le Crous, the art collector and critic. He just wrote a piece about the latest opening at the River Heights Museum of Fine Arts for the *Times*. Rufus, meet my friend Nancy Drew. She's River Heights's resident detective."

"Hello, Mr. Le Crous," I said.

Rufus touched his fingers together and made a triangle with his hands. His frown deepened, and his sleepy eyes nearly closed. "Hello, little sleuth," he finally said in a deep voice.

"I'm not little," I said, "but it's nice to meet you, Mr. Le Crous."

"Then perhaps you'll solve a mystery for me."

"I'll see what I can do. But first you have to tell me what the mystery is."

"Find out where the Duchess stashed the only worthwhile pieces in her measly collection."

"Oh, Rufus, I don't think that's something Nancy should bother with," Susan interjected. Turning to me, she said, "Rufus has a special interest in the work of D. Shammas. He came specifically to see the paintings in the Duchess's collection. He's rather upset that they aren't on display tonight. I told him the Duchess has a right to decide which pieces to share with us. After all, it's been ten years since she showed anything at all. But he's refusing to listen. Although he did come a long way to be here tonight."

Rufus Le Crous exhaled sharply, nostrils flaring. "Four hours in rush-hour traffic."

"Did you hear that a piece in the Duchess's collection was stolen last week?" I asked him. "A statue of the Roman goddess Diana disappeared during the grand opening of Angelica Velvet's new art gallery. Maybe the Duchess couldn't bear to lose another of her pieces to the same thief who stole her statue, and that's why she isn't showing the Shammas paintings."

"That would explain the extra security tonight," said Susan.

"The Duchess has delusions of persecution. *And* delusions of grandeur," said Le Crous, gesturing at the granite throne. "Peggy Guggenheim had a throne just like this at her palace in Venice. The Duchess's is a *poor* imitation."

"Surely it's not delusional for the Duchess to think her art might be in danger. After all, someone stole her statue in broad daylight in a crowded gallery just a few days ago," I said.

"I am aware of the theft of that Diana statue. It

was a trifle. A child's toy," said Le Crous dismissively.

"I heard it was ancient, like from Roman times. Mona Pearl said it was priceless."

"Priceless? Ha! Not according to my sources," Le Crous scoffed. "Like I said, the only worthwhile pieces in the Duchess's collection are the Shammas paintings."

"How do you know the statue isn't valuable? I don't understand why Mona Pearl would lie about that," I said.

"As a journalist, I must keep my source's identity a secret until my book has been thoroughly fact-checked. I don't want to risk a libel lawsuit. But let's just say that on the walls of the Strickland mansion, not all is as it appears."

"Who was this Shammas guy, anyway? I'd never heard of him until recently."

Le Crous spoke slowly, as if the words had come to him in a dream. His eyes had a distant, faraway look. "I know only these things about him: He was from the American Midwest. He painted in the 1990s. He only ever made four paintings, as far as my research can prove. But according to my sources, every one of those paintings was a masterpiece."

"What got you interested in Mr. Shammas?" I asked, trying to be polite. Le Crous reminded me a little of Mr. Covarrubias. They both had deep, plummy voices, and they both loved to hear themselves talk.

"I'd heard rumors of Shammas's first set of portraits for years. Word was that someone had offered ten million for the pair, but the anonymous seller refused the offer. That caught my attention. Then I'd heard a second set of Shammas portraits had ended up in the possession of a certain small-town Duchess. I had to see for myself whether these paintings were worth all the excitement, if, indeed, they existed at all."

"That's very interesting," I said, not really meaning it. Le Crous seemed to have two moods: grumpy and pompous.

"Through interviews with individuals who claim to have seen the portraits, I have been able to determine that Shammas was left-handed, and that he often painted and repainted a canvas hundreds of times before he considered it complete. All my findings will be detailed in my book, which will be released next year to major accolades and awards, not to mention blockbuster sales, of course. I already have interested publishers."

"Wow," I said. "Good for you, Mr. Le Crous." Fortunately, I was rescued from further small talk with the puffed-up writer by the hiss of microphone feedback.

A red-faced man in spats had climbed the stairs of the throne platform next to us, wireless microphone in hand. He was apparently suffering from a bad case of hay fever, but he made his announcement nevertheless, sniffling into the microphone. "Excuse me, ladies and gentlemen. *Ahem.* May I have your attention? I am Lesley Gatewood, the Duchess's personal secretary, and it is my honor to welcome you to the Strickland mansion for the first time in ten years."

The crowd cheered; some of the rowdier guests hooted like monkeys and howled like wild wolves. Mr. Gatewood waved his hands to quiet them.

"I see you're all suitably dressed. Most of you, anyway," he went on, watery eyes scanning the room. "This evening, the Duchess has graciously opened her home to you, her River Heights neighbors, alongside luminaries of the art world, performers, musicians, collectors, and curators. It is her belief that you all have something to learn from one another."

Some guests clapped. A few giggled nervously. Mostly, it looked like the River Heights citizens and the artsy visitors were keeping their distance from one another, gathering in little clusters of reserved folks or flamboyant outfits. Maybe the Duchess had some plan up her sleeve to help these two groups get to know each other. Lesley Gatewood sneezed three times in quick succession, then blew his nose into a lacy handkerchief, which he stuffed into one pocket of his immaculately tailored trousers before continuing.

"At eight o'clock the Duchess would like to share an announcement of her own. Until then, please feel free to enjoy our famous Strickland hospitality, view the art, and mingle. But please be assembled back here by eight for the Duchess's announcement. I promise it is not one you'll want to miss."

With a final, strangled cough, Lesley Gatewood switched off the microphone and yielded the stage.

Now the crowd was really confused. All around me, I could hear people murmuring to one another.

"Is the Duchess leaving River Heights?"

"I heard she's broke. Squandered her husband's fortune on paintings."

"I hope she donates some to the River Heights Museum of Fine Arts, at least."

"Maybe she's taking the whole collection to the dump."

I remembered Zeke's slip of the tongue. He'd said the Duchess was having an auction. Was that her big announcement—that she was putting her beautiful artwork up for sale? Why would she do that? How would Zeke have heard about her plans? And if she *was* auctioning everything off, why would she invite the citizens of River Heights? Most people I knew didn't have money to spend on huge, fancy oil paintings or marble statues for their gardens.

"What do you think the Duchess is up to?" I asked Susan.

"From what I remember, in the old days the Duchess used to love party games and icebreakers. She always sat strangers next to one another at her dinner parties to see if she could make them into friends over the course of the meal."

I had to admit that sounded pretty fun. Maybe there weren't any big mysteries to this party. I should try to enjoy myself and meet some new people.

But then, from across the room, I heard a shriek of fury. Angelica Velvet was advancing on Zeke, who was backing away through the crowd, palms raised. In the confusion, I saw Diana slide her tablet into her bag and slip through the crowd. From where I stood by the granite throne, I was perfectly positioned to spot Diana's angular haircut as she hurried through the ballroom doors into the main gallery, where she disappeared through a small door under a huge oil painting of a stormy sea.

I excused myself, telling Susan and Le Crous I had

to find my friends. "Fun talking to you, Mr. Le Crous!" I called. He frowned and shook his head.

As I crossed the room, I waved to Beverly DeSantos. Surely she could rescue poor Susan from Rufus Le Crous the Bore. Right now, I had other fish to fry.

The door in the hallway was marked with a small sign that read OFF-LIMITS TO GUESTS! Why had Diana ignored the sign? Was she on the hunt for the elusive Shammas paintings? And what would she do if she found them?

CHAPTER EIGHT

The Empty Pedestal

THE OFF-LIMITS DOOR LED TO A LONG hallway, its walls lined with pale green patterned wallpaper. Unlike the main gallery and ballroom, the walls of this hallway were not crammed with gold-framed paintings. In fact, the only things hanging along the hallway's entire length were five small oval-shaped portraits with modest wooden frames. The first portrait showed a pretty black woman in a simple green dress sitting before an easel and holding a paintbrush. Next was a shoulders-up portrait of a man with a prominent nose and tired, kind eyes, with just a touch of gray at his temples. Then came the profile of a teenage girl in a head scarf, and finally, two small portraits of toddlers, one with a huge floppy white bow on her head, the other dressed in a miniature sailor suit.

You could see that all the subjects were related; the sailor-suited child had the same nose as the older gentleman, and the girl with the bow had the same wide honey-brown eyes as the woman with the paintbrush. Though they weren't as showy as the paintings in the ballroom, these portraits looked important hanging there all alone. The Duchess probably looked at them every time she walked up and down this hallway. *This could be her family,* I thought. I squinted at the little toddler with the floppy bow, trying to imagine what she would look like as an adult. Was her hair parted straight down the middle? And who was that boy in the sailor suit?

The hallway came to an end at a wooden sliding door decorated with intricate carvings of leaves and blossoms. I slid the door back as quietly as I could and tiptoed inside.

Diana Yip stood with her back to me in a cozy drawing room. The walls were lined with bookshelves and decorated with medieval tapestries of unicorns that glowed ghostly white in the dim room, which seemed to have no windows to speak of. Four tufted armchairs and two love seats were arranged around a cold fireplace. The only light came from a spotlight, positioned directly above an empty white pedestal in the center of the room. That had to be the place where the statue of the goddess Diana had once stood. Rufus Le Crous had called it a child's toy, but the Duchess clearly thought differently, since the pedestal was in a place of prominence, just like the oval portraits in the hallway. It must have held something the Duchess valued immensely.

Moving as silently as I could, I hid behind one of the tapestries. Diana leaned close to the pedestal but didn't touch it. After a few seconds, she straightened up and walked very slowly around to the back, squinting as if she were trying to see some hidden detail from the right angle.

For a moment I imagined Diana Yip climbing up on that pedestal, striking a pose, and turning into a statue herself.

Don't be silly, I scolded myself. *Women don't just turn to stone.*

Suddenly Diana dropped out of sight. I pulled back the fabric, stretching to see where she'd vanished to without giving my own hiding spot away.

I could just make her out crouched behind the pedestal, tilting her head back and forth. What was she up to? Was Diana somehow involved in the disappearance of her goddess namesake? She had been so upset when they'd had to cancel the second half of the performance . . . but maybe she had her reasons for not wanting the show to go on. Even so, if she already had the statue, why would she try to steal a pedestal out from under the Duchess's nose? It seemed like a lot of work for a pretty unremarkable hunk of plaster.

And the pedestal seemed like it was pretty well-guarded. A gray box on the far wall looked like it might be a control panel for a security system. Black plastic bubbles were mounted in the corners near the ceiling—probably cameras. I waited for Diana to trip the sensors. She was so close to the pedestal, within arm's length. She reached out her hand and stroked the plaster surface. I braced for the shriek of an alarm, but nothing happened. Maybe the alarm was silent? I listened for footsteps in the hall, security guards rushing to defend the Duchess's property. Still nothing.

Diana was listening too. Now she knew the pedestal had no defenses.

I couldn't let her carry out whatever her mysterious plan might be right under my nose. I had to do something. Walking on tiptoe to keep my party heels from clicking against the marble floor, I slid out from behind the tapestry and tried to steel myself for a confrontation.

Just as I opened my mouth, Diana drew back her arm, balled her hand into a fist, and let fly a roundhouse punch to the side of the pedestal. The plaster gave way with a tremendous *CRACK* and the pedestal rocked on its base, then crashed to the floor.

I threw my hands over my mouth to stifle my cry of surprise.

Chief McGinnis and some of his officers were at the party just a few rooms away. I could have them back here in less than a minute.

But something about Diana's actions stopped me from revealing myself. She wasn't trying to steal the pedestal, not after she'd smashed it nearly in half. And I didn't really believe that Diana would sabotage her own performance and her friendship with Mona Pearl over a statue. No, Diana was rummaging around in the debris, *looking* for something. If I stayed quiet a few seconds longer, she would lead me right to it.

Still crouching, Diana took out her tablet and snapped a photo, then tapped out a message and hit send. I could hear the *whoosh* of the outgoing text. Was Diana sending Zeke a "Mission Accomplished" message? There had been something odd about the way he'd dodged my question back at Slay Gallery. A hint of self-satisfaction, like he knew more than he was letting on. It definitely seemed like he knew the Duchess. Was he the mastermind behind the art heist, with Diana acting as his accomplice? That didn't explain what I'd just witnessed. Why leave even more evidence behind? Especially evidence that could so easily be tracked. Diana's hands were probably covered in plaster dust, and she was leaving fingerprints everywhere.

Diana brushed plaster dust away from something in the debris and took several more photos, the shutter sound startlingly loud in the empty drawing room. *What kind of art thief forgets to silence her device before a heist?* I wondered. No, it just didn't make sense. I couldn't believe that shy, sad Diana Yip was involved in any sort of crime. But then how could I explain what I'd just seen?

Diana stood and slid her tablet into a pocket in her dress. There was something else in her left hand, but she hid it behind her back before I could see what it was. I froze, realizing too late that I was still standing out in the open. If Diana turned her head, even a little, she'd see me.

And as soon as the thought crossed my mind, she did exactly that.

"Nancy Drew, what are you doing here?" Diana's eyes were wide and frightened.

"Would you mind telling me what you just put into your pocket?" I asked.

She was silent for a long moment.

"It's nothing," she finally said, her voice barely a whisper. "Just an old sketchbook."

"Come on, Diana," I said, exasperated. "I saw you pull something out of the pedestal."

"You're a real gumshoe, Nancy Drew."

"I just want to know what happened to that statue," I said, moving closer.

"Then you'll have to ask someone else. I don't have a clue."

"An expert told me the statue wasn't even valuable. Do you know if that's true?"

"It was valuable to me. Mona Pearl promised I could have it after the show. It's mine."

"So you *did* take it?" I darted to one side, trying to catch Diana off guard, but she kept her face to me, backing toward the sliding door.

"No! Whoever took the statue didn't steal it from the Duchess. They stole it from *me*. I'm the only other person who could really appreciate that piece."

"Why's that?"

"Because I love the artist who made it. That statue tells me something about her, something she wouldn't say out loud. That's what makes it valuable. Not some expert's opinion."

"Okay, so who made the statue?"

Diana shook her head.

"You can tell me," I coaxed, reaching out to lay a hand on her bare arm, the same one twisted behind her back, protecting her hidden treasure. "I'm sorry, I have to go!" Diana's voice trembled. What was she so frightened of?

"You don't have to worry. Everything's going to be

all right. If the statue isn't worth anything, the thief will probably bring it back. A fake is no use to a thief. You'll get your statue back in no time."

Diana mumbled something, but I couldn't make it out.

"Excuse me?"

"I said, the girl detective hasn't cracked it yet." And then Diana made a break for it, scurrying out into the hallway, throwing the sliding door between us. I heard the clunk of a lock slipping into place. I yanked the handle as hard as I could, but the door stayed shut.

"Diana, let me out! Just tell me the truth. I promise you won't be in trouble," I called, but there was no reply.

I checked the time on my phone: 7:50 p.m. I had to make it back to the ballroom before the Duchess's announcement. By now, all the guests would be in the ballroom. Everyone, including the Duchess's granddaughter. If I could spot Mona Pearl in the crowd, I could ask her why she'd tried to pass off a fake statue as ancient and valuable art.

But first I had to get out of the drawing room, and the sliding door was stuck fast. It could be that there was another, hidden exit from the room. Before I started searching, though, it wouldn't hurt to examine the scene of Diana's sort-of crime.

I went back to where the pedestal lay on its side, surrounded by pieces of plaster and dust. Diana had left a fist-size hole in the side of the plaster, revealing a hollow center, a rectangular space large enough for a loaf of bread, a book, or a small painting. Before touching anything, I took out my phone to document the debris and saw I had three missed texts from George.

Where are you?

You're going to miss the Duchess's announcement!

Hello???

I'd text her back in a second and explain where I was. Then George could come and rescue me. She'd like that.

The hole in the pedestal had already revealed its secrets to Diana, but maybe she had left something behind. I covered my hand with a fold of my skirt so I wouldn't erase Diana's fingerprints, and felt around inside the cavity. My fingertips brushed something at the very back—something long, thin, and slithery, with a weight on the end. Not a snake, I realized as I pulled it out. A red ribbon with a charm on the end. I held it up to the light, watching the silver ornament spin. It was some kind of lizard—a tiny chameleon with a curly tail and tiny, glittering eyes made of red rhinestones.

The ribbon was pretty, but it was too short to wear in your hair.

"What are you for?" I wondered out loud.

Meanwhile, as the chameleon spun, I could've sworn it *winked*.

Then it came to me: a bookmark! The ribbon was the perfect length for sliding between pages, and the charm kept the ribbon in place.

Maybe Diana was telling the truth about what

she'd found. But if it *was* a sketchbook, who did the sketches belong to, and why was she so anxious to hide them from me?

I slipped the ribbon into my dress's smallest pocket for safekeeping. While I was writing a text to George, I heard someone in the hallway, struggling with the door.

I ran over to the door and pressed my cheek against the carved wooden flowers. "It's locked! Let me out!"

On the other side, I heard grumbling. The lock clunked open and someone pulled back the door. I'd hoped it would be George or Bess on the hunt or me, but I found myself face-to-face with Rufus Le Crous. The imposing man gave a high-pitched yelp of surprise at the sight of me.

"I was looking for the bathroom," he stuttered. His formerly puffed-up chest had deflated, and he was sweating profusely around the rim of his red cap. So Le Crous had a third mood: suspicious.

"It's in the main gallery. There were signs."

"Let's agree not to tell anyone we were here, yes?" said Le Crous.

"Why would we agree to that?"

"Because, Miss Drew, if we don't, I'll tell the Duchess you destroyed her property." He pointed first at the toppled and smashed pedestal, then at the plaster dust on the front of my dress.

"I didn't do that," I said.

"Of course not," said Le Crous. "I didn't do anything either. That's why no one has to know about it. Anyway, we're almost late to the Duchess's speech. Better come along." He grabbed me by the elbow and tried to escort me down the long hallway, but I wrenched my arm loose.

"I can walk myself, thank you." He shrugged and walked on ahead of me.

What was Mr. Le Crous doing poking around an off-limits part of the mansion? "Wait a minute. You were hoping to find those Shammas paintings you're so eager to see, weren't you?"

Le Crous turned around. "So what if I was? You

were obviously doing your own snooping. Find anything interesting?" He motioned toward the smashed pedestal.

"No, somebody else did. But you're right. We'd better get back to the ballroom."

Le Crous and I walked separately down the hallway back toward the gallery. I inspected the wallpaper's green pattern again and realized that the print wasn't abstract scrolls or chevrons like you'd expect in a grand home. Instead it was an interlocking design of tiny green chameleons, pulling one another along the wall by the tail. Chameleons just like the charm on the bookmark.

I nodded to each portrait as I passed by. First to the two toddlers, smiling in their cute outfits, then to the teenager, who looked straight ahead. I nodded at the kind older man, and finally, at the woman artist, whose face was turned just enough that our gazes met. She was smiling gently, as if she'd just had a wonderful idea. I tried to compose my face to match hers. It was strange—once I met her gaze,

I found it impossible to look away. I couldn't quite capture her expression. My lips wouldn't curl right, or my eyes were too crinkled. She stayed in the frame, perfectly composed, watching me.

Meanwhile, Le Crous had left me behind.

When he reached the door, he turned and saw what I was looking at and chuckled. "Come along, copycat," he said.

CHAPTER NINE

~✦~

The Duchess's Announcement

I FOLLOWED LE CROUS OUT INTO THE gallery, and then to the ballroom, which was packed with guests. The Duchess's staff bobbed and weaved in their red jackets, silver trays balanced high above the many heads. I couldn't spot Diana's sharp haircut anywhere, and there was no sign of Bess or George among the assembled guests.

The chandelier twinkled above me, trembling slightly from the movement of the people gathered below. I watched it sway, hypnotized by the way the crystals caught the light. The fixture had electric lightbulbs, but it also still had its original sconces, meant to protect flickering gaslight flames. In the center of the chandelier, I thought I saw a flash of pink material. I squinted. It looked like a big pink bow, tied as though it were a present. Why would someone go to the trouble of decorating something already so beautiful? I shook my head. Artsy people being extra artsy. Or maybe I was just dazzled by the lights.

Finally I saw Hannah in a knot of admirers, all gesturing at her fascinator. I giggled, struck by how perfect a name that was for the funny hat. Hannah caught my eye and waved me over.

"It's genius," said Mr. Covarrubias, stroking Hannah's arm. "The way you clustered the cherries . . . the visual sweep . . . you're a radical, a visionary!"

"I don't know about 'radical,'" Hannah said, beaming at the compliment.

"How did you make that fantastic shape?" asked a woman in a shimmering green sari. "It reminds me of an Elsa Schiaparelli design."

"Oh, Elsa!" Hannah exclaimed. "She's one of my idols. I love her work with Salvador Dalí."

"The infamous shoe hat!" crowed the woman in the sari, and the two of them burst into laughter like old friends.

"I always hated that hat," interrupted a male voice, followed by a prolonged bout of particularly disgusting throat clearing. Lesley Gatewood had appeared among us. He went on, "A woman's head is sacred. To cover it with a dirty old shoe! The nerve. Dalí was nothing but a fraud. But your hat is lovely. Like Philip Treacy, if he had an ounce of restraint."

"Oh, thank you, Mr. Gatewood. I think," said Hannah graciously.

But Gatewood wasn't finished. "The Duchess is on her way down to the ballroom now. Let us gather around the throne and make ready for her appearance."

"He thinks she's a real duchess," said the woman in the sari, her voice a stage whisper. "Should we all bow down?"

Gatewood sniffed but ignored the comment. He

began herding our group like a sheepdog, practically nipping at everyone's heels. I slipped away while he was distracted with Mr. Covarrubias, who had wandered back to the dessert table.

Finally I had a chance to finish my text to George: I'm in the ballroom. Where are you?

Three dots appeared at the bottom of my screen. George was typing. Then the dots disappeared.

I sent a question mark but didn't get a response.

A clock began to chime eight o'clock. It was time for the Duchess to reveal herself and tell us all why she'd gathered us in her mansion for the first time in a decade. Mr. Gatewood stood beside the throne with his arms tucked neatly behind his back. The crowd fell silent.

A string quartet began a dignified processional, heavy on the cello. I heard a breathy tune rising in accompaniment from somewhere in the crowd. The four flute players from Mona Pearl and Diana's performance appeared on the throne platform. They must have been mingling with the guests until the appointed moment.

Mona Pearl was *definitely* here in the room. But where? I hung back near the doorway, trying to scan the crowd in a methodical way, examining one head after another for Mona Pearl's distinctive dark hair, parted down the middle. Everyone was looking past me, toward the grand staircase outside the ballroom doors, where the Duchess would make her entrance.

We waited another long moment, every onlooker tense with anticipation. But when the Duchess appeared at the top of the staircase, she did not descend alone. She had an escort, a handsome young person in a blue tuxedo.

My friend George Fayne was holding the arm of River Heights's legendary Duchess Strickland. The two descended the grand staircase, one step at a time, slowly, and then crossed the gallery floor. The Duchess wore a dignified gown and a long green satin cape embroidered with curling vines around the edges. She really did look like nobility. I couldn't imagine how the two of them had met. George had probably been getting into mischief somewhere upstairs.

Maybe she'd been caught in the act, and playing the Duchess's escort for the evening was her penance.

But George looked so pleased with herself—I knew she couldn't be in trouble. Either way, she still hadn't replied to my text!

The crowd parted as the Duchess and George entered the ballroom. I caught a flash of bright green wool in the shifting crowd. Zeke was just across the room from me, huddled in conversation with someone who wasn't Diana. I didn't see the woman's face, but by her willowy dancer's build, her graceful arms and hands, her bizarre feathered breastplate, and most of all, her center-parted black hair, I knew she had to be Mona Pearl. From the way they bent their heads together, Zeke and Mona Pearl looked like old friends, like two people who'd known each other a long time. But just as soon as I'd seen them, the pair of artists melted away into the crowd.

The Duchess and George were passing before me, nearly to the platform. Close-up, the Duchess wasn't as grand as her named suggested. In reality, she was a tiny, hunched old lady with a twist of gray hair. Her wrinkled brown face lit up with a kindly smile as she looked out at her guests. She held up one knobbly hand and waved like royalty, but I saw that her fingers were covered in colorful splotches. How strange. Had the Duchess forgotten to wash her hands before her own grand party? That wasn't very elegant.

I'd seen a few weird things in the Strickland mansion that evening, but the strangest of all had to be the transformation of my clumsy, messy, tomboyish friend. Usually George couldn't be bothered to brush her hair, but now, with her head held high and her shoulders squared, helping the Duchess climb the stairs to her throne like a gallant knight, she actually looked the part.

Where was Bess when I needed her? I held up my phone, snapped a photo, and sent it to Bess with a row of confused emojis.

Mr. Gatewood scurried to the throne, dismissing George with a wave as he fussed over the seated

Duchess and handed her a microphone. George left the platform and rejoined the crowd.

A deep, powerful voice came from the old woman's throat. "Welcome, one and all, to the Strickland mansion. It has been far too long since I opened my home to guests. After my husband died, I hid myself away. I didn't want pity. I couldn't bear to be around people. These paintings and sculptures were the only companions I desired. I spent ten long years with my collection, at the expense of many things—friendship, community, watching my grandchildren grow up."

So Mona Pearl wasn't the Duchess's only grandchild. . . . I remembered the two small portraits in the off-limits area. The little girl must be Mona Pearl. So who was the boy in the sailor suit? If Mona Pearl was at the Duchess's party, so was he. And maybe we'd already met. . . .

I felt a pair of hands on my shoulders spin me around and bit back a shriek.

George was grinning so hard, I thought her face might split. "What'd I miss?" she asked.

"You're in high demand this evening."

"You wandered off first."

"Good point. How exactly did you meet the Duchess? I'm dying to know. Or are you too fancy to share secrets, now that you're a VIP?"

"No way. Just listen." She smiled and held a finger to her lips.

Duchess Strickland continued, "Only recently have I been made aware of just how much I missed. My grandchildren came to see me, though I did not wish to be seen. They convinced me it was time to let go of my silent beauties, my precious artifacts. They said I should donate the collection to a museum, or sell it off at auction. But I'm afraid I can be a stubborn old lady. It didn't feel right to sell my collection, which has been so much more than simple pictures and sculptures to me.

"Many have told me my plan is a poor one. Even my closest companions advised against it. And yet, here I stand. Here it is. I am giving away my entire collection. Tonight. One night only. Each piece will find its match. Mr. Gatewood, you will take it from here and explain how the distribution will work. . . ."

The Duchess handed the microphone back to her secretary. Gatewood accepted it with two reluctant fingers, as though he were touching something distasteful. The crowd rumbled, some disturbed, others gleeful. The River Heights citizens gathered around the platform, pleading with Mr. Gatewood to explain. Gatewood ignored them. He had tucked the microphone under one arm and was consumed with the task of polishing his glasses with his snotty handkerchief. We could hear the squeaking feedback from the trapped mic. Gatewood was stalling for time. I could see that now. He didn't seem to want the Duchess to go through with her plan. He must have been one of the close companions who had tried to talk her out of it.

And maybe he was right. The Duchess's plan did seem strange. Her collection was priceless, and it would be a huge loss to River Heights if the big-city guests took all the best pieces and resold them in their galleries for millions of dollars. I caught more than one guest scanning the walls with an appraising eyeball, considering which piece they'd take home. Or how many they could carry. Was this elegant party about to become a free-for-all?

CHAPTER TEN

Lights Out

WE NEVER GOT TO FIND OUT. BEFORE MR. Gatewood could speak, the grand chandelier shut off, plunging the ballroom into darkness. The lights in the gallery snuffed out all at once. Someone screamed, and the crowd panicked, stampeding the snack table, grabbing purses, and racing for the exit, where George and I were standing. I held on to the doorframe as people pushed past, pouring out into the gallery, where enough moonlight streamed in through the skylights that the blackout didn't seem as frightening.

I heard the Duchess's booming voice cutting through the noise.

"Lesley, help me down!"

"Coming, coming," replied Mr. Gatewood.

Chief McGinnis was hollering, trying to calm everyone down.

"Please stay where you are, everyone. I'm sure this is just a temporary outage, right, Mrs. Strickland? We'll get the power back on as quickly as we can!"

Duchess Strickland did not reply. Instead I heard scuffling—the sound of a large, ungainly object sliding over a smooth surface. Then something heavy slammed down. The crash echoed through the emptying space. What had fallen? Where was the Duchess now?

Someone shoved my shoulder from behind, pushing against the tide into the ballroom. I whirled around, but the person's face was in shadow and their body seemed to be entirely covered in a strange furry material.

"Excuse you!" I called out, but they didn't stop. I heard other people yelp, one after another, their complaints marking the shover's path through the darkness. Whoever it was, they were making their way toward the Duchess's throne.

"Is this a second art heist in progress?" I asked George. Even though I couldn't see her, I knew she'd replied with a shrug.

"I don't know. Why would someone rob the Duchess when she was going to give everything away for free?"

"Stop! Thief!" I called, but my voice was swallowed in the crush of frightened people pushing their way out of the ballroom. I heard something that could only be described as *slithering*, like the sound of a snake moving quickly through grass, or a satin ribbon coming undone. . . .

With the help of the security guards, his officers, and a lot more shouting, Chief McGinnis managed to corral everyone in the gallery. Gradually, the guests settled down into impatient complaining.

George and I stayed where we were, watching everything. Even if that rude stranger *was* an art thief, they wouldn't be able to carry anything out past us in the doorway and the crowd in the gallery. Unless there was another way out of the ballroom.

"Does anyone have a flashlight?"

"You animals tore my skirt! Don't you know this is *Dior*?"

"I'm calling my lawyer. You can't just go around telling people they can have things for free and then shutting the lights off! We live in a society!"

"I think it's thrilling . . . all of us here, in our finery, in total darkness. Why, almost anything could happen. . . ."

"Has anyone seen the Duchess?"

I heard someone hit a switch. The ballroom's central chandelier burst to life, flooding the room and illuminating Bess standing in the middle of the ballroom in her silver gown. She held a cake platter above her head. On it was a small, scrumptious-looking red velvet layer cake, molded in the shape of a heart.

Above her, Sven Svenstein, his lanky frame

squeezed into a silver-spangled leotard, dangled by one ankle from the chandelier on a wide pink ribbon. So I hadn't imagined that hidden bow. Sven must've prepared that early in the night while everyone was still arriving and the ballroom was empty. He was craftier than I'd given him credit for. And he knew his way around the Duchess's mansion. But how?

The Duchess's throne was empty, and there was no sign of her among the guests.

"Transformation! Revolution!" Sven bellowed.

With one arm, he held a shiny bugle to his lips. He took a deep breath and blew an earsplitting note. The guests in the hallway, curious to see what was going on, began filing past George and me in the doorway and back into the ballroom.

Below Sven, Bess lowered the platter and carved a bite of cake with a miniature gold fork. She had always prided herself on her impeccable manners. She lifted the fork to her lips. Even now, with everyone's eyes on her, Bess ate gracefully. The guests fell silent as Bess chewed daintily and dabbed the corners of her mouth with her napkin. She didn't even smudge her lip gloss. Between bites, she twirled her fork with an elegant flick of the wrist. The Duchess's guests murmured, some people admiring Bess's artistry, others confused by the demonstration. A few people even applauded, cheering Bess on.

I was fascinated by the crowd's reaction. Here was my friend, whom I'd known all my life, suddenly the center of attention, a performer. The big-city guests didn't seem angry at the interruption. In fact, most of them seemed amused. As the performance went on, people started to giggle, then titter. One onlooker doubled over with laughter, gasping, "Eat your heart out!" The River Heights citizens looked a little shell-shocked. I could understand that reaction much better than the laughter. The first evening at the Duchess's in a decade, and already we'd had enough excitement to last us another ten years!

"Bess is a star," George whispered. I nodded. She *was* a star, no doubt about it. The silver threads of her dress glimmered in the light. The audience was captivated. How long did a performance have to last? And how did you know it was over?

Bess cut another slice of the heart. We watched her eat until the whole cake was gone, devoured, without a crumb left. Bess swallowed the last bite, then flashed us a million-watt grin and dropped into a curtsy. The crowd burst into applause. Bess spotted us and ran over. George and I pulled her into a three-person hug.

"Bess, that was amazing!" I said.

"I was so nervous," she said, blushing. "I was worried people would think I was gross."

"That was a little weird, but pretty cool, Cousin," George said grudgingly.

"You eat like a queen," I added. Bess beamed.

Most of the guests had drifted back into the ballroom by now, and everyone seemed to be looking around for Mr. Gatewood to tell them this was all part of the celebration and they could take their free paintings now. But he was nowhere in sight, and neither were any of the red-jacketed staff.

Meanwhile, everyone assumed Sven's performance was finished. Boy, were we wrong.

Sven dropped the bugle, extracted a squashed roll of parchment from his leotard, and began to read a long speech about how art belongs to the people and shouldn't be held prisoner by criminals like their eccentric hostess, or power-hungry tastemakers like Angelica Velvet, or boring institutions like the River Heights Museum of Fine Art. He managed to offend pretty much everybody in about four minutes of monologue, which, I had to admit, was kind of impressive.

Nobody likes being lectured to, especially at a party, *especially* when the hostess and her staff have vanished. And I was learning that every performance had its limit. You can't perform your whole life long. Eventually the performance has to end, and you have to take off your mask and show everyone who you really are.

Rufus Le Crous was the first to start booing. I saw him at the edge of the crowd, pinching his nose as though he'd smelled something terrible.

"This is not art, you charlatan!" he shouted. "Come down from there at once!"

"You know nothing of my work!" Sven called back.

Others took up Le Crous's critique.

"He's only doing it for views. Ignore him and he'll go away."

"There's no money in performance art. It's a terrible investment."

"This isn't 1973. Get a new shtick."

"I say cut him down!"

"Funny sort of party favor. Is he meant to be a piñata?"

The spell was broken. People began to laugh and point. Cameras flashed.

"The performance is not over!" Sven cried, but the crowd ignored him. Several guests came up to congratulate Bess, as though she was the artist and Sven only her assistant. One elderly German even bowed to kiss Bess's hand.

"Wunderbar!" he said, his cheeks cherry red. In the background, the Duchess's staff returned, swarming around Sven with a ladder and untying him from the chandelier. He kicked and screamed the whole way down.

Bess stood still for a moment, thinking. Then I watched her square her shoulders and straighten her spine. George and I exchanged a look. We knew exactly what Bess was about to do.

Bess marched over to Sven. He was curled in the fetal position on the ballroom floor, murmuring to himself. George snorted. "He really looks like a baby." Bess bent down and laid a hand on Sven's shoulder. Though we couldn't hear what she was saying, Sven's face told the whole story. He was being dumped.

And just when it seemed like Sven's night couldn't get much worse, one of the police officers approached Bess and him, looking red-faced. The officer was clearly not happy about their little display, or the panic it had caused.

Meanwhile, Chief McGinnis was assembling a search party. It seemed that the Duchess had disappeared in the confusion. Mr. Gatewood was missing too. What had become of the stranger who shoved me on their way into the ballroom?

Bess walked back over to us, and I told her and George to hang out in the doorway. "I need you two to keep an eye out for Zeke or Diana Yip. And Mona Pearl. Text me if you see any of them in the gallery or the ballroom. And make sure Rufus Le Crous doesn't try anything funny. He'll say he's just looking for the bathroom, but don't listen to him. He's on a mission. And watch out for Angelica Velvet. She's hungry for drama. If the Duchess or Mr. Gatewood reappear, call me."

"Sure, Nancy. Is there anyone else we should watch for? D. B. Cooper? Banksy? Cinderella?" George quipped.

"Har, har. I think that's all my suspects. For now, anyway." Even if they didn't take it seriously, I knew I could trust Bess and George to help with my detective work.

I wandered back into the ballroom, moving quietly so as not to draw unwanted attention. The guests were gathered in small groups, discussing the events of the last half hour. The Duchess's throne stood empty under the light of the chandelier.

The Duchess and Mr. Gatewood couldn't have exited through the crowd or out the door, or I would've spotted them. George and I had been standing in the doorway. So it had to be the throne. . . .

I'd investigated mysteries in enough mansions to know their owners usually had at least one secret passageway or hidden door. Based on all the eccentric homes I'd visited in River Heights, I was starting to think the wealthy actually preferred creeping around inside the walls to spending time in their luxurious rooms.

I looked around to make sure no one was watching, then climbed the three wooden steps to the platform, just as the Duchess and Mr. Gatewood had done before the lights went out. I approached the throne cautiously, in case anyone was waiting to pop out from behind. No one did.

So I did something very bold. I took a seat on the Duchess's throne.

The seat was carved from a broad slab of polished stone. It wasn't very comfortable. I got up again and leaned forward to examine the edges, looking for a crack or knob, but I couldn't locate so much as a seam where the seat joined the back and arms of the gigantic chair. I knocked on the seat to see if it sounded hollow, then shook my hand, regretting the move. The stone was hard.

Was this a dead end? I was worried about the Duchess. If she'd vanished, just like her statue, would either of them ever be seen again? There were too many people at this party with hidden intentions. And the Duchess had said people had warned her against carrying out her plan. Had one of the Duchess's close companions been so desperate to stop her that they'd done something to her, using Sven's performance as a cover?

I slumped back down in the marble chair, kicking my legs and trying to think.

My heel connected with the base of the throne.

Click!

I jumped to my feet just as the seat and arms of the throne dropped away into darkness, leaving a gaping hole in front of the back of the chair.

I looked into the opening, trying to make out what was at the bottom. But the chandelier's golden light didn't reach into the darkness. I leaned a little ways into the shaft, trying to see better. . . .

And felt a pair of hands at my back. Before I could turn to see who they belonged to, I was shoved—hard. I tumbled over the edge of the opening and into the unknown.

CHAPTER ELEVEN

∾

The Strickland Family Business

ARMS FLAILING, I FELL FOR THREE FULL seconds—I counted under my breath—before I hit something solid. Fortunately, I landed on some sort of padded platform suspended in the shaft, which cushioned my fall. I didn't have time to save my phone, though—it fell out of my dress's pocket, slipped through a crack between the platform and the tunnel wall, and tumbled to its doom, crashing hard against a stone floor below. It looked like I'd been saved from a nasty fall. Far above me, I saw the small square of light from the opening that I'd fallen through, and then the square disappeared with a thud that echoed the length of the tunnel. That solved one mystery. The slamming sound I'd heard earlier before Sven and Bess's performance had been this seat slamming shut. Someone must have come down this secret passageway earlier. My assailant must have just closed the trapdoor, stranding me below. I didn't waste time wondering who had pushed me. That was a mystery to be solved later. First I had to figure out how I was going to get out of here.

I examined the platform that had saved me, which looked like a simple, open-topped elevator. The padded floor was enclosed by metal handrails, one side of which had a gate, a small ladder, and a control panel with up and down arrows. Beyond the gate there was an arched opening in the shaft wall, through which I could see a passageway lit by weak candlelight. There was no point in taking the elevator back to the top and pounding on the stone seat. It was solid marble. No one would hear me. The only way out was forward. I opened the gate and stepped through the archway, passing into a long, dark tunnel leading who knew where.

I could hardly see my hands in front of me. No phone meant no flashlight.

Maybe this tunnel leads to a secret art vault where the Duchess keeps her most valuable pieces, the ones she doesn't want to give away. Pieces like the two Shammas paintings?

Maybe...

Maybe it leads to the Duchess's wine cellar.

Maybe it leads out of the mansion completely—a secret passage that allows the Duchess to have groceries delivered without anyone knowing.

Maybe the Duke had a secret entrance so he could go from his home to work without having to face down angry bill collectors or unsatisfied customers. . . .

After what seemed like an eternity, I saw a small glow ahead—another candle flickering above a second open stone archway. I reached up and nudged the candle from its sconce. Then, holding the flickering candle flame out ahead of me, I pressed forward. I started to notice large rectangular shapes piling up against the walls on either side of me. Holding my candle closer, I saw that the shapes were stacks and stacks of canvases, unframed paintings, and stiff scrolls of parchment. I rummaged through a few of the stacks and noticed that most of the paintings were unfinished. The pictures were all different styles, but the unfinished ones were all unfinished in the same way.

The artist had started painting at the upper right corner of the canvas and worked his or her way down and over. But in all the unfinished paintings, the artist had left a bare patch of canvas in the lower left. The size of the empty spot told me how quickly the artist had gotten bored or dissatisfied with a painting and moved on to another idea, another canvas. I guessed the artist was left-handed, since they worked from right to left. That way, they wouldn't accidentally smudge the paint. Rufus Le Crous had said D. Shammas was left-handed too. Someone told me left-handed people were more creative, and right-handed people were better at solving problems. Was that really true? Maybe when I got back aboveground, I'd ask George to help me research how many other famous artists were lefties.

As I continued farther down the tunnel, the canvases multiplied, piled ten deep against the walls, making the space even narrower. I turned sideways to make my way past, and my skirt brushed against a stack, knocking away cobwebs, and maybe even setting a couple of spiders scurrying. And still, every unfinished painting had that signature bare patch of canvas. It looked like a lifetime's worth of work, false starts and variations. Some of the pieces were much more accomplished than others. Truthfully, I thought some were downright ugly.

I could tell when the painter had thought so too. The artist (or someone else) had painted slashes across the images in black paint. This detail, especially, convinced me I was looking at something other than a rich old lady's art hoard. The Duchess might be eccentric, but I had a hard time believing that she would invest her money in so many unfinished paintings. No collector would pay to have an artist deface pieces. There had to be another reason these canvases were here, stashed away like old love letters. . . .

Holding my candle close to the dusty floor, I could make out footprints—two sets. The first pair were the prints of tiny high-heeled shoes, with one print trailing into the next, like the person had been shuffling—the Duchess! Beside these was a set of larger, solid prints of a man's shoe. *Those must belong to Mr. Gatewood*, I thought.

They must have escaped the ballroom through the throne trapdoor—there weren't any other exits they could have slipped through without being seen. With the elevator at the top, it would have been easy to climb down onto it. Mr. Gatewood must have been holding up the Duchess's enormous cloak as they walked down the tunnel, or else it would have dragged on the floor. But where were they going? And why had they left? I'd have to ask.

The passageway turned left, then right, always

descending. I had to be much deeper than the mansion's foundations now. Finally the passage ended at a narrow staircase leading up to a door with another candle burning in the wall above it.

Mr. Gatewood stood at the top of the stairs, in front of the door, wheezing, hands on his hips, his face red as a tomato.

"Where does that passage lead?" I called up from the bottom of the stairs.

When he caught his breath, Mr. Gatewood pointed a forbidding white-gloved finger in my direction. "Miss! If you try to climb those stairs, I will be forced to stop you."

"Mr. Gatewood, are you threatening me?" I asked, shocked. The secretary had been prickly and pretentious all evening, but I'd never imagined he was hostile enough to cause anyone bodily harm.

"Not exactly," he said, wincing. He rubbed his hands together apologetically. "It's just that when the Duchess is working, she must not be disturbed for any reason."

"Working? Did she forget about her plan to give away her art collection? Upstairs, her party is in chaos. No one knows what's going on, and they had to cut Sven down from a chandelier," I said, stepping onto the bottom stair.

"Don't come any closer!" Mr. Gatewood tried to arrange his face into a threatening expression, but he just looked worried. He sighed. "People never appreciate the true value of the Duchess's work. I'm just glad she finally saw reason."

"What do you mean? Is the Duchess taking back her offer?" I climbed to the second step. Mr. Gatewood waggled his finger at me.

"Stay back!"

"Did you take the Diana statue from the Slay Gallery? Were you trying to frighten the Duchess into canceling her party?"

"I told her not to go through with her plan, but the Duchess is her own woman. When she ignored my advice, I simply took the liberty of bringing the Shammas paintings into the studio for the evening.

She's always worrying over them. But I never touched that amateurish statue. It's not even really the Duchess's, you know. It's Mona Pearl's." Gatewood sniffled.

"Why didn't you want anyone to see the Shammases, Mr. Gatewood?"

"If you have questions, you may ask the Duchess. But first, you must wait until she's finished with her work."

I decided to try a different tactic. Channeling Bess, I made my face as pleasant as possible and fluffed my dress. "It must be very hard for you. You've guarded the Duchess's work all your life, but nobody knows it."

Mr. Gatewood was seized with a fit of coughing. He doubled over and blew his nose extravagantly into a very damp handkerchief. When he stood again, I could tell I was making progress.

He smiled indulgently down at me and said, "She has these moments of inspiration. An idea comes to her, and she is compelled to bring it into being. Nothing can stop her. She inspires me. That's what I do it for, not the recognition."

"Do you spend a lot of time down here, Mr. Gatewood? These passageways must get gloomy."

"Actually, they're quite convenient, since we had the lifts installed. There are entrances all over the house, and they all lead here, all so the Duchess is never far from her work in progress. My employer is a woman of great focus and great intensity. You know, the only reason the Stricklands have anything at all is because of her hard work. It's a shame that *some* people in her family don't appreciate that."

"Oh? Who do you mean?"

"Edmonia, for one! Her own daughter! She thinks her mother is nothing but a— Well, I won't say it. But it's *very* disrespectful, considering all the beauty the Duchess has given to this world. You know, they haven't spoken in years, not since the incident with the Shammases. . . . But I shouldn't speak of such things. I'm just a gossipy old secretary. You can't know how terribly intrusive it feels, having to open our home to anyone who says they have an invitation. The Duchess is generous—far more generous than she needs to be."

I remembered the portrait from the off-limits hallway. The teenage girl must be Edmonia, Mona Pearl's mother. I was forming an idea that explained everything that had struck me as odd about the famous Strickland art collection, from the vanished statue to the secret passageways to the canvases in the hallway, the family portraits upstairs, and maybe even those two hidden Shammas paintings. But it was only an idea, and I needed facts. The only person who could confirm my theory was hiding just beyond the door, blocked for the moment by Mr. Gatewood's feeble frame.

"Listen, Mr. Gatewood," I said sweetly. "I know you have your orders, but I'm going into the Duchess's studio whether you like it or not. If we don't get her to come back to the party soon, people will start tearing paintings off the walls."

Mr. Gatewood let out an anguished cry and covered his face in his hands, racked by another coughing attack. I took the opportunity to climb to the top of the stairs and slide past him, turning the knob and passing into the central chamber: the Duchess's secret studio.

The cluttered octagonal room had a curved ceiling. From where I stood, I could see that there were seven other doors, one in each of the other walls. No doubt these led off to the Duchess's other secret passageways. Several worktables were covered with crumpled tubes of paint and worn-looking brushes, palettes clogged with dried paint, and rainbow-speckled washcloths. More unfinished canvases leaned against the walls.

Across from me, two easels stood side by side, each holding an enormous canvas. In the gap between them, I saw the Duchess perched on a motorized chair, the seat of which had been elevated so she could reach the top of the canvases.

I shuffled into her line of sight, waving awkwardly.

"Hi, Mrs. Strickland. Sorry for bursting in like this. I'm Nancy Drew."

"Enter, and call me Duchess," she said in her booming voice.

At that moment, Mr. Gatewood rushed into the

room. "I tried to stop her," he said in a rush. "She insisted on seeing you. I'm sorry, Duchess."

"It's quite all right, Mr. Gatewood," the Duchess replied. "I'd like to hear what she has to say."

"Of course, Duchess. Is there anything you require?"

"Bring fresh brushes, please," the Duchess replied before returning her gaze to me. Mr. Gatewood nodded and left through another of the studio's doors.

I made my way through the canvas graveyard to catch a glimpse of what she was working on. Each canvas was nearly a life-size portrait—one of a young man, the other a young woman—posed against a backdrop of vines, tropical flowers, and colorful birds. Were these the famous Shammas portraits?

I tiptoed around behind the Duchess's chair. She wasn't just looking at the Shammas portraits. As she reached for one canvas with her wrinkled hand, I saw that she was holding a long wooden paintbrush dipped in mauve paint. There was a tray attached to the arm of her chair that held a can of water, a selection of brushes, and a palette scattered with crumpled-up tubes of acrylic paint. With a few careful strokes, the Duchess adjusted the color of the young woman's cheeks, making them extra rosy. If these *were* the Shammas portraits, why would the Duchess try to "fix" them?

I understood when I got a better look at the face of the young man. It was Zeke, painted in minute detail. The likeness was unmistakable, down to his mischievous grin and bright green cloak. I didn't recognize the portrait of the young woman, but I knew it had to be Mona Pearl.

"Did you paint these?" I asked the Duchess in amazement.

She hummed to herself and kept painting. After a moment she said, "Five long years, and I still can't get them quite right. These paintings are the most precious pieces in my collection. Do you know why?"

"I think so. They're portraits of the two people you love the most—your grandchildren."

"That's right, Miss Drew. I need to make sure every last detail is perfect, because tonight I'm giving them to their rightful owners. This is the second set of portraits I've painted of my grandchildren, in fact. I painted them first as toddlers. You might say those portraits were the first originals I ever made."

"Your first *originals*? Does that mean you've made fakes?"

I looked around the studio, full of half-finished canvases. Could they all be the output of a single artist—the frail old woman sitting before me? What about all the works upstairs that made up the Duchess's priceless collection?

The Duchess dropped two brushes into the can of water and looked directly at me. Her honey-colored eyes twinkled merrily in her wrinkled face. She didn't seem angry that I'd found her out—far from it. She pressed a button on the arm of her high-tech chair, and with a whir, the seat descended from its elevated position and swiveled to face me.

"You see, I'm quite the chameleon. It won't be long before everyone knows. But for now . . . welcome to my studio," she said.

"Um, thank you for having me. You know, forgery's a crime—"

"Before you accuse me, know this: my husband was a failure. Poor, sweet, foolish Duke. He had many good ideas, but never a great one. The lace-making machine he invented made a small fortune, but it was soon replaced by faster machines and bigger factories. Then we found out the cat toys he created were a choking hazard, and his bottled tea recipes made people sick. He lost money on other investments too and landed himself in deep debt with bad people."

"But my dad told me Duke was River Heights's very own Thomas Edison."

"That's what my husband wanted everyone to think. All along, it was me keeping his businesses afloat by selling my work. If I hadn't done so, we would've lost our home, our daughter's college savings, everything."

"But how did you know selling forgeries would work? How did you avoid getting caught all these years?"

"I didn't know it would work, but I had no choice. When Duke's money troubles were at their worst, I had just given birth to our daughter and couldn't go to work. Instead I pored over art history textbooks and spent hours in museums, sketching from the masters, painting pictures over and over again until I got them exactly right." The Duchess gestured to the stacks of unfinished canvases around her. "It was an expensive hobby, but selling replicas paid off in the end."

"When did you start passing your work off as the real thing?"

"I didn't do it on purpose. I had taken one of my paintings to the city to be framed. A little something in the style of the Dutch masters, a still life of tulips and a dead hare, I think it was. The woman at the framing shop was so taken with the piece. She said she knew someone who would pay good money for it. Duke and I were drowning in debt at the time, so I let her sell the piece for me. Anonymously, of course."

"That woman—was it Angelica Velvet?"

The Duchess nodded solemnly. "She was convinced

the painting was genuine, and I suppose I never corrected her. Before I knew it, we were in business together."

"Didn't you ever feel bad that you were passing your work off as authentic?"

The Duchess rested her chin on her tiny fist and considered the question.

"I tried selling my own work, but because of Duke's reputation as a failed businessman, nobody wanted to give their money to a Strickland. Not even for my beautiful paintings. It was only when I assumed another artist's name that anyone noticed my skill. Those few originals I made, I signed under another name."

"D. Shammas," I said.

"Smart girl. Angelica Velvet knew lots of wealthy people who didn't ask questions. When she heard about my Shammas paintings, she begged me to sell them. She said she had a buyer who'd pay ten million dollars for paintings by the mysterious genius. But I wasn't ready to reveal myself or to give up those works. Those paintings are about my life. I could never sell them. Angelica didn't want to hear that, not at all. She said if I wouldn't sell the Shammas paintings to her, she was finished with me. So I gave her a few studies, but I immediately regretted it. After that, I never sold another painting, original or otherwise."

"Did Angelica know that the paintings she sold for you were forgeries?"

The Duchess shrugged. "It's funny. When I was working with Angelica, I never felt guilty. It was what I had to do to keep my daughter fed. I just wish Edmonia could understand that. When my daughter Edmonia was growing up, we never told her how our family made its money. She knew I could paint, but she was always more interested in her father's work. She spent all her free time in his workshop, tinkering. It was only years later, when she saw those little portraits, that she put two and two together. Edmonia was so angry. She said I'd made a fool of her father and that she'd never forgive me. She kept my grandchildren away from me for many years. That hurt, because I knew Ezekiel and Mona Pearl would become real artists. My grandchildren inherited my talents. They are both true originals."

"You can say that again," I said, thinking of Zeke's edible poetry and Mona Pearl's bizarre costumes.

"After they'd both graduated from high school, Edmonia couldn't stop them from visiting me. So Ezekiel and Mona Pearl came to stay for the summer. Mona Pearl took an art class. Ezekiel spent every afternoon in my library, devouring book after book. I painted a second set of portraits, these ones you see here. It was a special time."

"How long ago was that, Mrs. Strickland?" I asked.

"Oh, about five years ago. They discovered my studio right away, of course. Ezekiel was horrified. But Mona Pearl loved the idea of fooling people. I tried to tell her I had only done it out of necessity, to keep the family together, but she wouldn't listen. She said she wanted to continue the family business. I couldn't allow that to happen. We argued and Mona Pearl stormed out, followed by her brother. They never set foot in my house again. Until tonight."

"Until tonight—wait a second. Didn't you know Mona Pearl took the statue of Diana from your drawing room last week?" I said.

"Oh, was that her? I thought Mr. Gatewood had taken it to be cleaned. Well, it's her right."

"What do you mean?"

"That statue belongs to Mona Pearl. I've been looking after it for the last five years. It wasn't very well guarded. I think I always hoped she'd come back for it. What did she want with it?"

"She was going to use it in some kind of performance at the new Slay Gallery. But it disappeared in the middle of the show, and no one has seen it since!"

"Oh yes, now that you mention it, the police did call me to let me know the statue had been taken. I wasn't that concerned. It'll turn up, I'm sure. The things we make have a habit of coming back to us.

Besides, I'm too old to worry about such things anymore. That's why I threw this party in the first place. I'm finally ready to come clean." The Duchess bowed her head.

She sighed, her eyes sad and tired. Then she raised and swiveled her chair back to the canvases. "You'd better go on back to the party now, Miss Drew. I'd like to finish Ezekiel's portrait in peace."

Mr. Gatewood appeared through one of the eight identical doorways and presented the Duchess with a bouquet of paintbrushes, some fluffy, some stiff, with long wooden handles.

My studio visit was finished. How could the Duchess be so unbothered? I planted my feet right where I stood and spoke loudly. "Mrs. Strickland, I have to tell you something—your grandson and his friend stole from you too. I saw Diana Yip break into the pedestal where you used to display your missing Diana statue. She took something out of the pedestal and hid it in her dress. Zeke must have told her where to find it. I tried to confront her, but she got away."

The Duchess turned sharply in her chair. I took the ribbon with the chameleon charm from my pocket and dangled it on its ribbon.

"I think the two thefts might be connected," I went on, ignoring the Duchess's glare.

The Duchess took a long moment to respond. "If what you're saying is true . . . it means Diana found my ledger book. Only my family knows where I keep it. Only my family knows what's written inside. Only my family could have stolen it from me."

"What's in the ledger book?" I asked.

Mr. Gatewood stood still as a lizard, or maybe a chameleon.

The Duchess held me with her icy stare for a long time before speaking. "That book . . . is where I recorded the name of every person who bought or sold my work, and how much I made from each sale—everyone who ever fell for my fakes. It's a long list. If it ever got out, I'd be ruined." The Duchess smiled ruefully as she said it. One wrinkled eyelid fluttered. Was the Duchess winking? "Let's hope it doesn't get out."

"Yoo-hoo, Grandmother, are you in there?" called a familiar voice. I peeked out from behind the canvases to see Zeke, Diana, George, and Bess tumble through one of the eight identical doors.

CHAPTER TWELVE

A Low-Speed Chase

"NANCY, YOU'RE SAFE!" BESS CRIED. "WHEN you disappeared from the ballroom, we thought you might be in terrible danger!"

"I had a little fall, but I'm all right."

"Ezekiel!" the Duchess exclaimed.

Zeke bent his lanky frame to plant a kiss on his grandmother's cheek.

"Who have you brought with you? You know I don't allow just anyone into my studio."

"This is the lovely Bess Marvin and my dear friend Diana Yip." When Zeke said her name, Bess blushed a fetching pink. "I think you already know George."

George bowed. "A pleasure to see you again, Duchess," she said.

"Ah yes, my charming escort. You'd better tell me why you're here."

Diana Yip spoke up first. "I thought Zeke was crazy when he told me about your ledger book. He said you'd made a whole career as a forger, but I couldn't believe you'd even gotten one fake painting past the experts at the auction houses. But then I found the proof hidden in the pedestal in your drawing room, just where Zeke said it would be."

"Whoa!" said George and Bess in unison.

The Duchess looked sad. "I regret deceiving people, but it was what I had to do. May I have my ledger book back, please?"

"I'm sorry, Grandmother, but . . . no, you can't," said Zeke.

The Duchess looked at him, shocked.

Mr. Gatewood advanced on Zeke and Diana,

spluttering with rage. "How dare you disrespect your grandmother!" he shouted. "Give her the book this instant, or I will take it from you by force!"

"We can't give the book back, because we don't have it," Diana said.

The Duchess groaned. "You haven't lost it, have you? Imagine what would happen if that book found its way into the wrong hands!"

"No, Grandmother, we didn't lose it. The book is in good hands," said Zeke.

"Whose hands?" demanded the Duchess. I couldn't help thinking in the moment that it was the perfect name for her.

Rufus Le Crous had been in the off-limits hallway just after Diana Yip had locked me in the drawing room. Could he have been there to make a handoff with Diana?

I turned to Diana. "You gave the book to Rufus Le Crous, didn't you?"

But it was Zeke who answered, with a mischievous smile. "There's no sneaking anything past you, Nancy Drew."

"That's right!" said George proudly. "She's the best sleuth in River Heights, and probably the whole state!"

Now it was my turn to blush. But I was worried, too. Could the pompous writer really be trusted with a secret as earth-shattering as the Duchess's forgery career?

"Then you must be the top-secret source Rufus was talking about earlier. What is Rufus going to do with the ledger?" I asked.

"Publish it, of course," said Zeke. "It's time everyone learned who the *real* D. Shammas is. Rufus included."

"Do you actually think that's a good idea? Once the collectors find out they've been fooled, they'll probably want to sue the living daylights out of your whole family," I said. "And just think what Angelica Velvet will say! Or does she already know? Zeke, was that why she was arguing with you in the ballroom earlier?"

"Angelica believed in my grandmother's work when nobody else did. She has an eye for talent, there's no denying that. But she's gotten greedy, and out of touch. She freaked when she found out about my little publishing project. Said I'd ruin her. What Angelica doesn't know is this: the art world will forgive nearly any crime, so long as the work is interesting. Forgeries can be recast as masterworks, and vice versa. It's all a matter of perception. It took me a long time to come to terms with what my grandmother did, but I see her in a different light now. I believe, with my poetical skill, I can help others do the same."

"Will the art world forgive you for stealing your grandmother's statue?" retorted George. "We know you're the ones who took it."

"George!" I chided. "We don't know that. I told you, Diana only said that the statue was hers, not that she took it."

"I didn't take the statue. Even though it was rightfully mine," said Diana quietly.

"Of course you didn't steal it. But who promised it to you?" Bess asked sweetly, trying to coax Diana out of her shell.

"Mona Pearl did. When we were still collaborators. I don't know what we are now."

"But didn't that statue belong to the Duchess? It's one of her creations, right?" Bess asked.

"Mona Pearl made it herself, actually," the Duchess explained. "That summer she stayed with me. She was trying to prove that she could be just as good a forger as I was. I tried to convince her to focus on her own work instead of copying other people's."

"The Duchess isn't the only artist in this family," replied Zeke, chuckling. "She's just the only one to achieve major art world recognition. Not as herself, of course. When I received her invitation, I knew she wanted to change that. But giving away the paintings isn't enough. Grandmother, if you want to be recognized as the great artist you are, you have to tell the truth."

"But Zeke, don't you think people will be angry when they find out they spent all that money on fakes?" I asked.

"Art lovers appreciate any story that brings a little intrigue to their day," Zeke said. "Forged paintings and vanishing statues are *very* intriguing. And the whole story is even better: a mysterious artist turns out to be local philanthropist and collector Duchess Strickland! Rufus Le Crous may not be a pleasant man, but he's an excellent writer. If anyone can spin a good yarn from this situation, it's him."

"Why didn't you tell me about your plan?" asked the Duchess.

"I was going to explain the whole thing before you gave away your entire collection. But I had Diana give Rufus the ledger book first, in case you disagreed with my methods." Zeke turned to address me again. "Grandmother supports Mona Pearl and me as fellow artists. Even if we couldn't see her own art for what it was."

"That's right, Ezekiel," the Duchess said from her chair. "If I were fifty years younger, I'd start again as a performance artist."

"I think you've *always* been one, Grandmother," Zeke replied, resting a hand on hers.

"We should give the Stricklands a little time to talk this out, don't you think, Nancy?" Bess ventured, gazing shyly at Zeke. I could see she'd already moved on from her last artistic beau. "I'd like to get back to the party."

"Save me a dance, Bess?" asked Zeke.

"Of course!" She beamed.

"I agree with Bess," I chimed in. "If none of you took Mona Pearl's statue, I'd like to find out who did."

The Duchess pointed to the door to her right. "That one will take you back to the main gallery. I'll join you shortly, once my grandson sees fit to explain his master plan."

Mr. Gatewood took Diana's arm and shooed all of us toward the door.

"Diana can stay," Zeke said. "She's basically family, anyway, even if she and Mona Pearl aren't getting along right now." Diana smiled.

Mr. Gatewood reluctantly released her arm and sniffed, waiting for my friends and me to leave. "Don't breathe a word of where you've been," he said. "Please."

"We'll keep the Duchess's secret," I told him. "For now. Anyway, I still have one more mystery to solve."

"Thank you, Miss Drew," said the Duchess. She gave us a regal wave, and Mr. Gatewood ushered Bess, George, and me through the doorway into yet another winding passageway crammed with the Duchess's unfinished masterpieces.

The passage let us out through a revolving doorway cleverly hidden behind one of the gigantic rose-filled urns that flanked the staircase at the end of the main gallery. We approached the ballroom to find that the party was back in swing. The lights were on, and thankfully, nobody else was dangling from the chandelier. Chief McGinnis was pacifying some disgruntled out-of-towners, but the people I recognized from River Heights were mainly sitting back to enjoy the show. This was probably the most exciting party they'd been to in years!

I cast a glance over my shoulder, at the bare space on the wall where the Shammas portraits used to hang. Sitting on the bench before them was a sad figure with his head in his hands. It was Sven, having changed from his spangly leotard into a somber navy-blue one. Bess hurried past him without a glance, no doubt thinking of her promised dance with Zeke. I caught George's arm to get her attention.

"Can you guys see if they still have those little tea cakes? I never got to try one," I said, motioning George on ahead. I had a hunch as to who'd taken Mona Pearl's statue. Maybe I'd known it all along.

George gave me a look. "Okay . . . What are you up to, Nancy?"

"Just tying up some loose ends. Don't worry, I'll be there in a sec."

I went over to the bench and sat down beside the dejected artist.

"You stole the statue, didn't you?" I said gently. "Angelica Velvet let you into the gallery before the performance, and you hid the statue in your studio."

Sven did not reply. His face was stony.

"What was part two of your performance tonight? Where are you keeping the statue?"

When he still wouldn't respond, I tried one more

time. "That statue means something to you, doesn't it? Because you cared for Mona Pearl, and you know she made it. Do you still have feelings for her?"

Sven glared at me, then shook his head.

"All right, have it your way. I wanted to do this nicely. Now I'll have to find the statue and expose you as the thief."

"You just try it, Nancy Drew," Sven finally said. Without another word, he stood and slunk away toward the exit.

I heard the scrape of stone on stone. Mr. Gatewood emerged from behind the urn, followed by Diana Yip, Zeke, and the Duchess.

"Everything all right?" I asked them.

"We seem to have come to an agreement," said Mr. Gatewood curtly.

"I have one more announcement to make," the Duchess said, winking at me. "Come!"

I followed their procession into the ballroom. As the Duchess made her way through the crowd back toward her throne, people broke into spontaneous cheers and applause. The four bearded flute players from Mona Pearl and Diana's performance struck up a merry tune and were soon joined by the string quartet. With the Duchess settled on her throne once more, the crowd celebrated with dancing. Flamboyant out-of-towners grabbed hold of River Heights citizens and began to waltz. The man with the antlers spun Riley the photographer in a pirouette. I spotted Hannah Gruen twirling on the arm of Mr. Covarrubias.

Ahead of me, Bess ran up to Zeke and held out her hand.

"Zeke, shall we dance?" she asked.

He laughed. "Of course!"

I felt a tap on my shoulder. "May I have this waltz, milady?" George asked.

I decided the missing statue and Sven's come-uppance could wait until the song was over, so I fluffed my skirt and took George's arm.

I expected some awkward shuffling, and maybe a bow, but George turned out to be a surprisingly smooth partner, leading me through the one-two-three steps of the dance with ease. But because she was George, she also insisted on speaking in a British accent that was decidedly more chimneysweep than courtly gentleman.

"I learned from YouTube videos," George confessed. "I 'ad to practice for *hours*."

"Oh, Prince George, you're an absolute delight!" I said, giggling at my own terrible accent. As the song ended, I heard clapping off to my left. Someone was calling my name—Dad! And Ned, just behind him, both looking dapper in freshly pressed tuxedos.

"I hope you saved a dance for little old me," said Ned.

"Hmm . . . I think I just can squeeze you in," I said, smiling.

I hugged them both, but before I could ask my dad how their case was going, the music stopped and the tinkling of a bell cut through the sudden hush of the room. The Duchess stood before her throne, holding the microphone again. Was she finally ready to tell the truth?

Before the Duchess could speak, the lights flickered.

I heard the sound of thunder approaching.

"What now?" someone groaned.

"Not another interruption!" complained someone else.

Everyone was nervously watching the chandelier. We heard shouting from the main hallway, and the squeal of rubber against stone.

With a roar like a thousand angry lions, Sven came screeching into the ballroom astride his art cycle, a hideous machine encrusted with torn bits of painted canvas, silverware, stuffed animals, fast-food wrappers, fake flowers, tennis balls, plastic jewelry, and other colorful junk. He'd changed from his navy-blue leotard into another skintight outfit made of shiny purple spandex. Attached to the cycle's handle-bars was a three-foot-tall statue of a woman with a crescent-moon headdress, holding a metal bow with a real arrow.

The room exploded in an uproar. People climbed over one another, trying to get out of the art cycle's path.

"Stop that at once!" the Duchess shouted into the microphone.

But Sven ignored her, barreling toward us. I realized the goddess's arrow was pointed straight at me!

George must have realized it too. She tackled me to the ground, James Bond–style.

"Oof!" We rolled to safety under the dessert table.

Just before he crashed into the table, Sven slammed on the brakes and threw the cycle into reverse. He peeled backward out of the ballroom, shouting, "Yes, it was I who took your precious, worthless statue! I exposed your fakery, which is the fakery of all artists! It's impossible to be original! Art is theft and theft is art! Come and get me, Nancy Drew!"

When we were sure Sven wasn't circling back to flatten us, George and I crawled out from under the table.

"I know Sven was just being dramatic, but he was actually right on with all that fake art stuff," said George, blinking.

"Wow, George. I never thought I'd hear you say

Sven was right about anything," I replied. She shrugged.

Guests were straightening their outfits and tsking over Sven's dangerous performance. Bess came running over, anxious to make sure we were okay.

"Oh, Nancy, your dress is all dusty!" she cried.

"Don't worry about that right now, Bess. It's up to us to rescue the goddess!"

My friends and I had to chase Sven down before he destroyed the statue.

"We're coming too," called Zeke and Diana, rushing to our sides as we followed Sven out the front door.

"Fine. There's no time to waste arguing," I said. "Everyone'll just have to squeeze into the hybrid."

I ran over to the valet stand and asked for my car.

"Make it quick, please!" I urged the young valet.

He brought the car around as fast as he could, and George, Bess, Zeke, Diana, and I all squeezed in, Bess taking the opportunity to scooch close to Zeke. I slammed my foot down on the accelerator and sped down the gravel driveway as fast as my little car could go, which wasn't as fast as I would have liked.

Before we came to the gate, I spotted a patch of disturbed gravel up ahead. Skid marks veered off to the left, into the trees.

"Looks like Sven didn't get far after all," I murmured.

I turned off my headlights and pulled slowly off the driveway and into the woods. My passengers were as quiet as mice, watching intently for any sign of the fugitive.

We followed the tracks to the edge of a small clearing, where I saw a figure hunched over the smoking wreck of the art cycle. My hybrid's electric motor was perfectly silent as we snuck up on the scene. The figure's back was turned to us, but it had to be Sven. Nobody else would wear a skintight leotard like that. Sven's shoulders shook. Was he crying?

"Wait here," I said to my friends. "And if I say run, start the engine!"

"I'm coming with you," said George.

"Me too," said Bess. "I don't want to miss anything good."

"So are we," said Diana. "Duh."

"All right," I said reluctantly, "but stay quiet and follow my lead."

I flicked the headlights on, illuminating the clearing, then got out of the car. Sven spun around, and I saw that he wasn't crying—he had been struggling to lift the heavy statue from the art cycle's wreckage. Having successfully extracted it, he held Diana out in front of him, skinny arms trembling.

"Come any closer and the goddess gets it!" Sven yelled.

He thrust the statue away from his body, and I saw that he was holding it out over the sharp crags of a large boulder. If he dropped the statue now, it would shatter into a million pieces.

CHAPTER THIRTEEN

❧

The Artist Revealed

"DON'T DO IT, SVEN!" BESS CRIED.

"Come on, man," Zeke chimed in. "That's my sister's work. She made it when she was just a teenager. You've made your point. Now give it back."

Sven ignored them both and let the statue slip through his hands, catching it by the waist again just before it hit the boulder.

Diana let out a tiny scream. "Please be careful!" she begged.

"My hands are getting sweaty," Sven said, grinning evilly. I knew there was only one way to distract the artist long enough to rescue the statue. I'd have to ask him about his art.

"What *was* your point, Sven? What are you trying to say?" I asked in a curious, polite voice.

He looked at me for a long moment, his brow furrowed. "I am trying to tell the truth, Nancy Drew," he finally said. "Obviously."

"Yes, but what truth is that?" I pressed. "You talk about truth and revolution all the time, but I don't know what that actually means. What do you want your art to be? Because destroying someone else's sculpture isn't a good look."

"Ha! By destroying Mona Pearl's fake, I will be more of an original than she could ever be!"

"Actually," George interrupted, "destroying art isn't all that original. In the 1950s, Robert Rauschenberg erased one of Willem de Kooning's drawings and called that art. In the 1990s, the Chinese artist Ai Weiwei took photographs of himself dropping and breaking a two-thousand-year-old urn from the Han Dynasty."

Sven glared at her.

"I *hate* art history," he grumbled.

"So let's have it, Sven. The truth," I said, crossing my arms. "We can wait."

"You really want to know?" Sven asked.

"I really do," I said gently. "This isn't about revolution at all, is it?"

"No," he said glumly, sitting down on top of the boulder with the statue wrapped securely in his arms. "It's about Mona Pearl."

"It's okay. You can tell me," I said, tiptoeing closer.

Sven heaved a dramatic sigh. "It's hard, being a lone genius. I know that I intimidate people. But I don't want to be alone. All my life, I've wished for nothing more than a good collaborator. The only person I ever thought was worthy, the only person whose talent matched—even outweighed—mine, didn't want me. She went away to the big city and found someone she liked better. And then she had the nerve to come back to River Heights to show off that perfect partnership right in front of me. And in my mother's gallery, where *I* was supposed to be the star! I couldn't stand it."

"Wait a second. Angelica Velvet is your *mother*?" I said, stunned. I took the opportunity to plop down next to Sven on the boulder, which was not very comfortable.

"No way," said Bess. "Last week you called her 'the establishment'!"

"She is," said Sven matter-of-factly. "But she promised to help me out. I've been spending a lot of cash on old TV sets. I may be broke, but at least I've got the key to the hottest gallery in River Heights." Holding the statue with one arm, he reached into the neck of his leotard, pulled out a string, and dangled a large silver key before my eyes. "Literally."

So Angelica Velvet had given Sven access to the gallery before the show. If she knew about the theft, she certainly wasn't going to report her own son. That explained why she was so quick to blame Mona Pearl and Diana Yip for their failed performance, and also why she was so cagey when we met at the entrance to the Strickland mansion. Goodness, was everyone in the art world secretly *related*?

"It's not fashionable to talk about taking your parents' money, but lots of artists—the successful ones, usually—have a little help. My mom wants me to make a name for myself. It's a lot of pressure sometimes," Sven said. He gave a little shrug of his shiny shoulders.

"I can understand that," I replied, laying a hand on his free arm. "But your mom doesn't know everything."

Sven let out an unhappy sob and clutched the goddess tight to his chest.

"Oh, Sven, you'll be all right. Give us the statue. I promise, you can still be an artist. You just have to give up on this particular piece, okay?"

Zeke leaned against the boulder on Sven's other side and put an arm around Sven's shoulder. "My sister is making a name for herself with her own ideas and her own talent," he said. "That was my grandmother's dream for us. And you know better than anyone that art is for dreaming. Give us back the statue now and we won't report you. You'll be free to keep doing . . . whatever it is you do."

Sven considered this offer. His grip on the statue loosened. After a moment, he allowed Zeke to extract the goddess statue from his grasp.

We returned to the ballroom just in time to hear the Duchess resume her speech. We'd left Sven behind to mourn his art cycle. Mr. Gatewood was testing the microphone and watching the chandelier with a concerned look while the Duchess soothed worried guests from her throne. Zeke was carrying the goddess statue on his hip like a baby. Bess followed behind him, watching appreciatively. Diana was smiling for the first time all night. The Duchess saw us coming and waved us up the steps of her throne platform.

"I am happy to see you all," she said, beaming. She looked at the statue on Zeke's hip. "And *you*, especially, Diana. Well, I suppose it is time for the world to meet the woman behind the mask. It is time for the truth."

We assembled behind the throne and the Duchess

stood to address her audience, everyone who had witnessed and appreciated her lifelong performance. Mr. Gatewood handed her a microphone.

"An hour ago," she began, "I nearly called off the whole evening. I was unhappy with my work, and afraid that no one would appreciate it as it really was. I wanted to send everyone home. And I would have! But a brave young woman came to see me, and she helped me change my mind. You know, I think she reminded me a little of myself when I was young. So, my beloved guests . . . Let me begin by presenting a metaphor."

The Duchess gave the microphone back to Mr. Gatewood. *So she has one last trick up her sleeve, after all,* I thought. The Duchess really was a performer.

She crouched down and pressed what I could see now was a hidden button in her throne to open the trapdoor. The bearded quartet took out their flutes and played a single chord. When they fell silent, something rose through the throne's trapdoor. A huge, misshapen figure, its face obscured by a tall collar of woven sticks, followed by gloved hands and a body covered in patches of brightly colored fur. It was the masked dancer, Mona Pearl!

Now that I was watching the performer close-up, I could see that what I'd previously thought were twigs and branches were actually paintbrushes—hundreds and hundreds of them—glued together to make her tall collar.

The audience watched, enraptured, as the masked dancer climbed out of the throne and took the stage, swaying in that same hypnotic dance she'd done at Slay Gallery. She danced for a minute, then fell still, her masked head bowed.

The Duchess applauded and the crowd joined in. Mona Pearl took a bow, and then slowly, carefully, removed the collar.

Beneath was a beautiful young woman, a few years older than me. She had honey-colored eyes, a black waterfall of curls parted straight down the middle, and skin the same shade as the Duchess's. She was the same woman I'd seen talking to Zeke when the Duchess and

George were making their entrance. And she looked just like her portrait. Mona Pearl turned her back to the audience. She was looking straight at us—at Zeke, who was still holding the goddess statue. She held out her arms for it, and Zeke handed it over.

Mona Pearl embraced the statue, spinning on tiptoe like a ballerina. She kept spinning, moving closer and closer to Diana, who was already giggling. The crowd clapped louder, as if this was all part of the show. When Mona Pearl was dizzy, she stopped, planting her feet right in front of Diana. She held out the statue, swaying slightly.

"I'm sorry for all the dumb stuff I said earlier. You're my collaborator. I should've listened to you. I know I can trust you to tell me the truth."

Diana accepted the statue, her round face blushing. Though her voice was quiet, I heard her say, "I forgive you, Mona Pearl." They hugged the statue together, both grinning like crazy.

The crowd, confused but understanding that the statue's reappearance in the Strickland mansion was undoubtedly a good thing, gave another round of applause.

"Champagne!" somebody yelled.

"More dancing!" cried someone else.

"More cake!" yelled Bess.

Mr. Gatewood grabbed the microphone and cried, "Shhh!" There was a screech of feedback.

When the crowd settled, the Duchess drew Zeke and Mona Pearl to her side. "Ladies and gentlemen, thank you for your patience. And now, as promised: the first gift of the evening. To my grandchildren, Ezekiel Romare Strickland and Mona Pearl Primus Strickland, a pair of invaluable Shammas portraits."

Behind her, Mr. Gatewood, huffing and puffing, hauled the two portraits up through the throne trapdoor on a special pulley system.

"Nobody touch! They're still wet!" he cautioned.

Mr. Gatewood displayed the freshly finished portraits beside Mona Pearl and Zeke. The crowd looked on, murmuring in amazement at the painter's skill and gradually making the connection: the subjects of the portraits were standing before them. Duchess Strickland had revealed the family secret.

"That's right, ladies and gentlemen. *I'm* D. Shammas," said the Duchess. "And every painting you see here—every painting in my collection—they were all created by the same artist. The one and only Daisy 'Duchess' Strickland."

At that moment I spotted Angelica Velvet in the crowd. She had changed wigs since I last saw her, and was now wearing a severe black bob and hexagonal glasses with red frames. The assistant from Slay Gallery hovered at Angelica's elbow, watching her anxiously. A muscle twitched in Angelica's jaw. It was impossible to tell if her expression read as anger or amusement, fear, or satisfaction.

"What is the meaning of this?" yelled the mustachioed man in the kimono. "Are you telling me I spent half my inheritance on fakes?"

"How droll!" said the man with the antlers, toasting to the chaos.

"Let's hear her out!" shouted Mr. Covarrubias.

In the commotion, Mr. Gatewood climbed down onto the platform beneath the Duchess's throne and reemerged carrying a pile of canvases. As he unstacked the paintings and set them out one by one, faceup on the stage, he looked unhappy but resigned.

"Don't worry, he always looks that way," whispered Zeke.

"Thanks to my dear, creative, hotheaded grand-children, my art will find a new life without the mask," the Duchess continued. She spread her arms toward the crowd. "And so, let us begin. To my grandson, Ezekiel Romare Strickland, I give his sister's portrait, and to my granddaughter, Mona Pearl Primus Strick-land, your brother's portrait, so you remember that a loving family is also a work of art. I know you think I'm losing my mind, giving things away. But they're *my* things. I made them. All I ask is the power to decide who looks at them."

Mona Pearl smiled with tears in her eyes. Zeke nodded and threw a long arm around the tiny Duchess. I could see the younger Stricklands were both proud of their talented, tricksy grandmother. In the crowd, Angelica Velvet whispered to her assistant, who nodded frantically and scribbled something in a notepad. She didn't seem concerned that her entire career had just been exposed as a scam. Maybe Zeke was right. Angelica was already thinking of a way to use the Duchess's unmasking to her advantage.

"I accept the consequences of my actions," the Duchess continued serenely. "If the collectors sue, let them sue. I'll pay back every cent they paid me. All I care about now is healing my family."

The Duchess gave her grandchildren another squeeze. "Rufus Le Crous, step forward, please. I believe you have something of mine."

Le Crous did as he was told, holding the Duchess's ledger book above his head.

"Journalistic privilege," he said smugly. "I already photographed several key sections and sent them to my publisher. You can't stop the truth from getting out."

"I don't want to," said the Duchess. "In fact, I encourage you to publish the whole thing. And I offer myself for one-on-one interviews, on any subject you like. In exchange, I'd like a cowriter's credit on your new book, of course."

Even a man as pompous as Rufus couldn't give up such a big scoop. He nodded and bowed low, clasping the book close. "Madam, I am at your service. Consider me your scribe."

"Lesley, if you would be so kind. Please distribute my wealth among our honored guests.

"To Ms. Hannah Gruen, my copy of Matisse's 'Woman with a Hat,'" she said. "You were the talk of the party.

"To Mr. Covarrubias, my entire collection of Greek and Roman statuary to use as models for his art classes.

"For Abby Heyworth, a scrumptious still life, all vegetarian, of course.

"To Angelica Velvet, I am sorry I can't make you any profits. I hope you will accept this painting of a dollar bill, inspired by Andy Warhol."

Angelica Velvet let out a sharp, barking laugh but accepted the gift, tucking the small painting away under her caftan. "My dear Duchess, we're long over-due for tea," she said. "Shall we make an appointment to plot your reentry to the art world?"

"Gladly, Angelica," said the Duchess, beaming. "I'm glad to be working together again."

The man with antlers was given a painting of a magnificent stag standing before a smoky moun-tain range. The four women in sequined coveralls were gifted a yellow-and-blue lithograph of four can-can ladies in the style of the French artist Henri de Toulouse-Lautrec. Maria the librarian was given a reproduction of a page from *The Book of Kells*, a beautiful illuminated manuscript originally made by monks in the ninth century.

"To Bess Marvin, a portrait of a French noble-woman who could be her double with those bright blue eyes.

"To George Fayne, a reproduction of the Artemisia Gentileschi painting *Judith Slaying Holofernes*."

"Whoa, this painting rules!" George exclaimed as Mr. Gatewood presented her with the framed artwork.

When everyone in the room had been given a painting of their own, the Duchess announced that the River Heights Museum of Fine Art could have everything that was left.

But there was one person who hadn't received a piece of the Duchess's collection. Me.

"And last, but not least, Nancy Drew," the Duchess said. I realized she was waiting for me to come and stand before her.

The Duchess's face, up close, was much softer and kinder than it looked from her throne, or glaring down at me from her mechanical painter's chair. Her honey-colored eyes twinkled as she laid a wrinkled hand on my arm.

"Dear Nancy, you have the clearest eyes of anyone here tonight. You saw me for who I really am. I see the creative spark in you, as I saw it in my grandchildren long ago. And so I bequeath to you a blank canvas, and my favorite set of brushes."

"I'm touched," I said, happy to be recognized for my skills of observation. I guess solving mysteries is an art form too. Though it was still bothering me that I didn't know who'd pushed me through the throne's trapdoor . . .

I gathered up the supplies, preparing to return to the crowd, but the Duchess wasn't finished. She leaned in close and whispered so that only I could hear.

"Please, my dear, make sure you always sign your work with your own name. I promise I'll do the same. From now on, anyway."

I nodded. As I returned to the dance floor and my friends, Mona Pearl came running after me.

"Nancy, wait! I want to apologize for pushing you. I'm sorry! I heard you talking to Officer Gutierrez after my statue disappeared. I knew you, of everyone here, would understand that my grandmother isn't a criminal. She's simply a great artist. I was trying to give you a little shove in the right direction."

"Goodness! I thought you were trying to kill me! You really should have checked whether the platform was there," I said. "But you were right. It took a little while, but I do see the Duchess as an artist. An amazing one! I just hope she makes amends to the people she swindled. Forgery is still a crime, after all."

"My grandmother is finally ready to live as herself. Thank you for helping her tell her story." Mona Pearl leaned down and kissed my cheek. She smelled of tropical flowers. Her hair brushed against my cheek, and I saw it was pinned back with a bumpy green barrette. But it wasn't a barrette at all—it was a live chameleon, sitting in a nest of her dark curls. I took the ribbon with its tiny chameleon charm from my dress pocket and dangled it above Mona Pearl's head. The chameleon reached out one horny green foot and grabbed the silver charm.

"Oh, don't mind Basquiat," said Mona Pearl, laughing. "He just loves beautiful things."

Dear Diary,

A FEW MONTHS LATER, RUFUS LE CROUS and the Duchess published an excerpt of their book in a premier art journal, revealing the true identity of the mysterious D. Shammas. They included the list of her work, and Zeke wrote a long poem that told the story of her life.

Using her connections in the art world, Angelica Velvet was able to spin the Duchess's career of deception as a long-running piece of performance art. Some of the owners were angry that their "originals" turned out to be fakes, but the good publicity convinced a lot of them to lend their pieces for a Daisy "Duchess" Strickland career retrospective at the River Heights Museum of Fine Art, and now the paintings are even more valuable!

Zeke and Mona Pearl's mother finally forgave the Duchess, and now they're all planning to spend the summer together at the Strickland mansion. I'm glad I could help the Duchess reconnect with her family. I got some nice paintbrushes in the bargain too. Now I just have to decide what to paint!

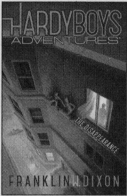 

Looking for another great book?
Find it
IN THE MIDDLE.

Fun, fantastic books for kids
in the in-be**TWEEN** age.

IntheMiddleBooks.com

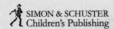